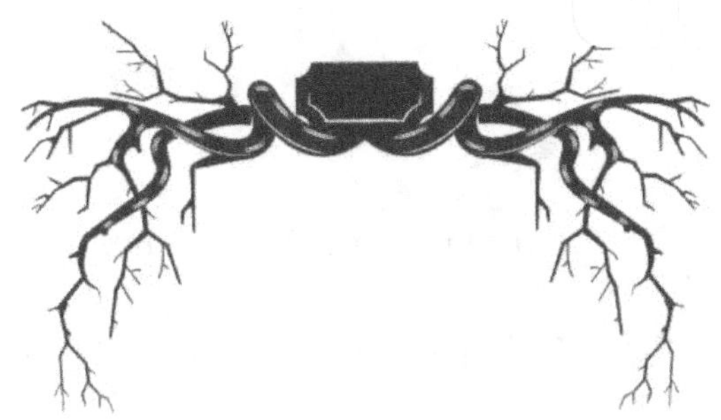

LEGENDS
OF THE
PRIMAL DAWN:

AGE OF STONE

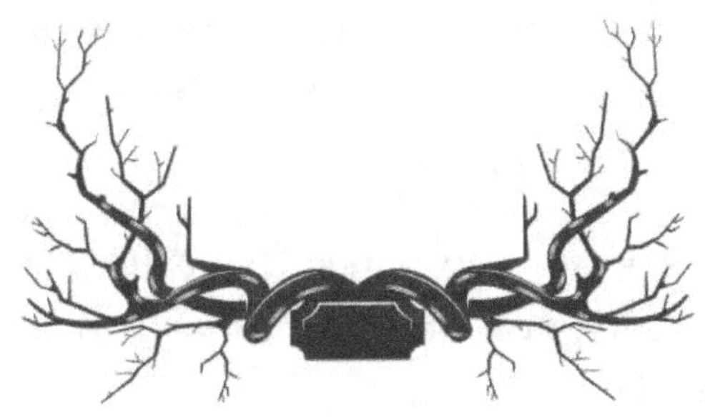

Acknowledgments

Writing this LitRPG adventure has been a journey filled with challenges, late nights, and moments of pure creative joy. But no journey is ever walked alone.

First and foremost, to my wife, Melody—your love, patience, and unwavering support have been my greatest strength. Thank you for believing in me, for understanding when the story pulled me away, and for always being my anchor in reality.

To my incredible children, Detra and Ivan—you inspire me every day. Your curiosity, laughter, and boundless imagination remind me why stories matter. I hope one day you'll embark on your own great adventures, whether in books, games, or life itself.

To my parents, who instilled in me the value of hard work, perseverance, and the love of a good story — thank you for shaping the person I am today. Your lessons and encouragement have never gone unnoticed.

And to my friends — those who listened to my ramblings about plot twists, mechanics, and world-building, and who never hesitated to lend an ear or offer a word of encouragement — thank you. Your support means more than you know.

This book exists because of all of you. I hope it takes readers on an unforgettable journey, just as writing it has done for me.

— Gerald George.

TABLE OF CONTENT

CHAPTER 1

THE AWAKENING

The air was warmed and rustled with an energy that felt both foreign and familiar, a sensation that jolted Jelani awake. He blinked against the harsh light filtering through the canopy of towering trees, their leaves shimmering like emeralds. A cloud of confusion settled in his mind as he pushed himself up from the damp earth. Where was he? The last thing he remembered was the bustling streets of Johannesburg, surrounded by the hum of city life.

Jelani took a deep breath, filling his lungs with the earthy scent of moss and wildflowers. He was no longer in the city; he was in a lush, prehistoric forest teeming with life. The sounds of chirping birds and rustling leaves enveloped him, but something deeper stirred within his chest - a calling.

As he stood up, he noticed others scattered around him. A woman with long black hair knelt beside a stream, her fingers tracing patterns in the water. Nearby, a tall man with broad shoulders examined a strange stone etched with symbols. Each face bore a mix of bewilderment and determination.

"Hey!" Jelani called out, his voice echoing in the stillness. "Does anyone know what's happening?"

The woman looked up, her dark eyes wide with surprise. "I'm Mei Ling," she said, rising to her feet. "I don't know how we got here either."

The tall man turned, revealing a chiseled jaw and intense gaze. "I'm Kofi," he said, brushing dirt from his hands. "We need to figure out where we are and how to survive."

As they gathered together, Jelani felt an inexplicable connection to these strangers—like threads woven into a tapestry yet to be completed. "We should explore," he suggested, glancing at the dense forest surrounding them. "There might be food or shelter nearby."

With a nod of agreement, they set off deeper into the woods, each step stirring excitement and trepidation within Jelani's heart. The forest was alive; vibrant colors danced around them as they moved through shafts of sunlight piercing the canopy.

Suddenly, a low growl soared behind a cluster of bushes. The group froze as a massive creature emerged - a sleek, muscular beast resembling a lion but larger, its golden fur glowing in the dappled light. It surveyed them with piercing amber eyes.

"Run!" Kofi shouted as he grabbed Mei Ling's arm and pulled her away.

Jelani's instincts kicked in; he pivoted on his heel and sprinted alongside them. The creature lunged forward, its powerful legs propelling it toward them with terrifying speed. They dashed through the underbrush, branches whipping against their skin as they fled.

"Over there!" Mei Ling pointed toward a rocky outcrop ahead. They veered left and scrambled up the slope just as the beast lunged again, narrowly missing Kofi's leg.

Breathless and trembling, they reached the top and turned to face their pursuer. The creature paced below them, growling softly as it circled like a predator waiting for its moment to strike.

"What do we do now?" Jelani panted, heart racing.

"We need to find a way to defend ourselves," Kofi replied, scanning their surroundings for anything useful.

As they caught their breath, Jelani felt an unfamiliar sensation wash over him — a whispering presence that seemed to resonate within him. It was as if someone — or something — was guiding him.

"Listen," he said suddenly. "I can feel… something calling to me."

Mei Ling's eyes widened in realization. "Ancestral spirits," she murmured. "It's possible we're not just lost; we might have been brought here for a reason."

Before they could ponder this further, the creature let out an ear-splitting roar that echoed through the valley. They were not just survivors; they were part of something much larger than themselves.

CHAPTER 2

THE GATHERING ALLIES

The day was filled with uncertainty. The sky was blue with hope. A little later, the sun dipped low in the sky as shadows lengthened across the forest floor. Jelani's heart still raced from their narrow escape, but curiosity began to overshadow his fear. He looked at his companions—Mei Ling's brow furrowed in thought and Kofi's jaw clenched in determination—and felt a surge of purpose.

"We need to find others," Jelani declared, breaking the tense silence that had settled among them. "If we're going to survive this place, we can't do it alone."

Kofi nodded in agreement but added cautiously, "We should also be careful. If that beast is any indication of what lies ahead… we need to be prepared."

Mei Ling stepped forward, her voice steady despite the uncertainty swirling around them. "Let's head toward that ridge," she suggested, pointing toward a

distant rise where trees thinned out into open ground.
"We might find higher ground or another path
leading out of this forest."

As they made their way toward the ridge, Jelani couldn't shake the feeling that they were being watched - an unsettling sensation that crawled along his skin like tiny ants marching across his body.

When they reached the ridge's summit, they paused to catch their breath and take in their surroundings. Below them sprawled an expansive valley dotted with clusters of trees and glimmering streams winding through lush grasslands.

"Look!" Mei Ling exclaimed suddenly as she pointed toward movement in the distance - a group of figures gathering near a fire pit surrounded by large stones.

"They look like people," Kofi observed cautiously. "But are they friend or foe?"

Jelani squinted against the fading light and felt an instinctual pull toward them - a sense that these individuals might hold answers to their predicament.

"We have to approach carefully," he suggested. "Let's see if we can learn more about them before making ourselves known."

They descended cautiously down the ridge toward the fire pit where shadows danced against flickering flames. As they drew closer, Jelani could hear snippets of conversation - fragments of stories filled with laughter interspersed with solemn tones.

"Do you think they'll help us?" Mei Ling whispered nervously.

"We won't know until we try," Kofi replied firmly.

As they approached the gathering under cover of darkness, Jelani felt an overwhelming sense of destiny wash over him—an awareness that this moment would shape not only their survival but also their understanding of who they were meant to become in this strange world.

Just then, one figure turned sharply toward them - a tall woman adorned in intricate beads and animal skins who seemed to sense their presence before they even stepped into view.

"Who goes there?" she called out sharply, her voice carrying authority that demanded respect.

Jelani stepped forward hesitantly but resolutely raised his hands in peace. "We mean no harm," he said clearly. "We're lost travelers seeking refuge."

The woman narrowed her eyes but gestured for them to come closer. As they stepped into the circle of firelight, Jelani could see other faces watching intently - some curious, others wary.

"I am Amara," she introduced herself after assessing them for what felt like an eternity. "And you are far from home."

"Yes," Mei Ling replied softly but confidently as she stepped beside Jelani and Kofi. "We were brought here without explanation."

Amara studied them closely before speaking again: "You are not alone in your journey; many have been drawn here by forces beyond our understanding." Her gaze shifted toward the darkening sky as if sensing something ominous approaching.

"The night is filled with dangers you cannot yet comprehend," she continued gravely. "But together… perhaps we can uncover our purpose."

As Amara spoke those words, an unsettling chill swept through the air—a harbinger of challenges yet to come—and Jelani knew that whatever lay ahead would test not only their strength but also their very souls.

Feel free to provide feedback or request any specific adjustments you'd like!

CHAPTER 3

THE CIRCLE OF ANCESTORS

The fire crackled, sending sparks into the night sky as Jelani, Mei Ling, and Kofi settled among the gathering. The warmth of the flames contrasted sharply with the chill that had begun to seep into the air, a reminder that danger lurked just beyond the flickering light. Amara sat across from them, her presence commanding yet inviting, as she began to weave a narrative that would shape their understanding of this strange world.

"Many moons ago," Amara began, her voice low and melodic, "this land was alive with the spirits of our ancestors. They walked among us, guiding our hands and hearts. But a darkness fell - a malevolent force that sought to erase our history and enslave our souls."

Jelani leaned forward, captivated by her words. "What is this darkness?" he asked, his curiosity piqued.

Amara's expression darkened. "It is an ancient evil known as the Shadow Wraith. It feeds on fear and despair, twisting the very fabric of reality. It seeks to rewrite our past and control our future."

Kofi frowned. "And you believe it has brought us here?"

"Indeed," Amara replied. "You were chosen for a reason. Each of you carries within you the blood of great ancestors - warriors, scholars, healers. Your strengths will be tested, but together you may have a chance to confront this darkness."

Mei Ling exchanged glances with Jelani and Kofi, a mix of apprehension and determination swirling in her eyes. "What do we need to do?" she asked.

Amara gestured toward the fire pit where a series of stones were arranged in a circle. "We must perform the Rite of Connection - a ritual that will awaken your ancestral abilities. Only then can you begin to understand your purpose in this world."

Jelani felt a surge of energy at her words, an instinctive knowing that this was what he had felt calling to him earlier. "What does the ritual entail?" he inquired.

"It requires each of you to confront your past," Amara explained. "You will enter a trance state where your ancestors will guide you. But be warned - the journey may reveal truths that are difficult to face."

Kofi looked skeptical but intrigued. "How do we know it will work?"

Amara smiled faintly. "Faith is a powerful ally in these woods. Trust in yourselves and in each other."

As the group prepared for the rite, Jelani felt a mixture of excitement and fear bubbling within him. He had always been drawn to stories of his heritage - tales of Zulu warriors who fought bravely against invaders - but now he was about to step into those legends himself.

"Sit in a circle," Amara instructed as she arranged herbs and stones around them. "Hold hands and close your eyes."

They complied, forming a tight circle as Amara began to chant softly in a language that resonated deep within Jelani's soul. The rhythm of her voice melded with the crackling fire, creating an atmosphere thick with anticipation.

As they breathed together, Jelani felt his heart rate slow, his mind clearing as if a fog was lifting. Images began to swirl behind his closed eyelids - visions of vast savannahs under an endless sky, warriors clad in traditional attire charging into battle against overwhelming odds.

Suddenly, he was no longer sitting by the fire; he was standing on that savannah, feeling the heat of the sun on his skin and the wind whipping through his hair. He looked down at himself and saw not his modern clothing but traditional Zulu garb - colorful beads adorned his neck, and a spear rested firmly in his hand.

"Jelani," a voice called out from behind him.

He turned to see an imposing figure approaching - a tall man with strong features and wise eyes that seemed to hold centuries of knowledge.

"Who are you?" Jelani asked, awe-struck by the presence before him.

"I am Shaka," the man replied with authority that resonated through Jelani's very being. "I am your ancestor."

Jelani's heart raced at the revelation. "Why have you come?"

"To guide you," Shaka said firmly. "You stand on the precipice of destiny - a destiny shaped by courage and wisdom."

As Shaka spoke, images flooded Jelani's mind - battles fought for freedom, alliances forged with neighboring tribes, moments of triumph and loss that defined his lineage.

"You must remember who you are," Shaka urged. "Your strength lies not only in your body but also in your spirit."

Suddenly, Jelani felt a jolt as if lightning coursed through him; he could sense power awakening within him - a connection to his ancestors that transcended time itself.

"Embrace it!" Shaka commanded as he raised his spear skyward.

Jelani followed suit instinctively; energy surged through him like wildfire as he channeled ancestral strength into his being.

As he stood there on the savannah under Shaka's watchful gaze, Jelani felt an overwhelming sense of purpose wash over him. He could hear distant drums echoing through the air - a rhythmic heartbeat that called him forward.

"Come!" Shaka beckoned him toward a gathering of warriors silhouetted against the horizon. They stood tall and proud, their bodies glistening with sweat from battle preparations.

"What is happening?" Jelani asked breathlessly as they approached.

"The time has come for you to join us," Shaka replied solemnly. "You will learn what it means to fight for your people - to protect those who cannot protect themselves."

As they reached the warriors, Jelani felt their energy enveloping him - a fierce determination radiating from each one like flames igniting within his own heart.

"Today we honor our ancestors," one warrior shouted passionately while raising his spear high above his head. "We fight not just for ourselves but for those who came before us!"

The crowd erupted into cheers; their voices echoed across the plains like thunder rumbling through storm clouds gathering overhead.

Jelani's spirit soared alongside theirs; he could feel every heartbeat resonating within him as if they were all connected by invisible threads woven throughout time itself!

But then something shifted - the air grew heavy with tension as dark clouds rolled across the sky obscuring sunlight filtering down upon them all now casting shadows over everything below!

"What is happening?" he shouted again desperately seeking answers amidst chaos unfolding around them!

"Beware!" Shaka warned urgently while pointing toward ominous figures emerging from shadows lurking just beyond reach! "The Shadow Wraith approaches!"

Jelani turned quickly; fear gripped him tightly like icy fingers wrapping around throat constricting breath escaping lungs! He saw twisted forms rising up from ground - dark silhouettes cloaked in swirling mists swirling around them obscuring faces hidden beneath hoods shrouded entirely!

"They come for us!" another warrior yelled while raising weapon readying himself for battle against impending doom looming ever closer now threatening everything they held dear!

"Stand firm!" Shaka commanded fiercely while drawing forth spear prepared defend against encroaching darkness threatening consume all light surrounding them!

But before any further action could be taken - a deafening roar erupted shattering silence echoing throughout battlefield sending tremors coursing through earth beneath feet trembling violently beneath weight crushing down upon spirits fighting valiantly against overwhelming odds stacked high against them all!

Jelani felt panic rising within, his chest pounding fiercely, demanding release. Yet, somehow, he held his ground, refusing to succumb to the fear tightening around his heart.

It threatened to pull him away from everything he cherished, but he clung to it desperately. Deep within, his soul yearned to break free from the chains that bound him, locking him away in the shadows - just beyond reach.

CHAPTER 4

TRIALS OF SPIRIT

The fire crackled softly, its embers glowing like tiny stars against the darkness of the night. Jelani sat back, his breathing still uneven as he processed the vision he had just experienced. The power of his ancestor, Shaka Zulu, still coursed through him like a river of fire. He felt stronger - more connected to something ancient and unshakable. Yet, questions lingered in his mind. Why had they been brought here? And what role did their ancestors expect them to play in this strange, perilous world?

"What did you see?" Kofi asked, his deep voice breaking the silence.

Jelani turned to him, his expression a mixture of awe and determination. "I met my ancestor," he said slowly, as though speaking the words aloud might make them more real. "Shaka Zulu. He... he showed me what it means to fight for something greater than myself."

Mei Ling's eyes flickered with curiosity and a hint of apprehension. "Was it frightening?" she asked softly.

Jelani shook his head. "Not frightening... but overwhelming. It was like standing in the presence of a storm - powerful and unrelenting."

Amara watched them silently from across the fire, her gaze steady and unreadable. She seemed to be weighing their words, assessing their readiness for what lay ahead.

"I want to try," Mei Ling said suddenly, her voice firm despite the uncertainty in her eyes.

Amara nodded approvingly and gestured for Mei Ling to take her place at the center of the circle. The others shifted slightly to make room as Amara began arranging herbs and stones around her in a precise pattern.

"Close your eyes," Amara instructed gently. "Focus on your breathing. Let the rhythm of the fire guide you."

Mei Ling obeyed, her hands resting lightly on her knees as she drew in slow, deliberate breaths. The air around her seemed to thicken, charged with an energy that made Jelani's skin prickle. Amara began chanting again, her voice low and melodic, weaving through the night like a thread binding them all together.

Jelani watched intently as Mei Ling's expression shifted from concentration to serenity. Her breathing slowed further, becoming almost imperceptible as she sank deeper into the trance.

Suddenly, Mei Ling gasped sharply, her body stiffening for a moment before relaxing completely. Her head tilted slightly as though she were listening to something only she could hear.

In her mind's eye, Mei Ling found herself standing in an ancient library unlike any she had ever seen before. Towering shelves stretched endlessly into the distance, filled with scrolls and tomes bound in leather that seemed to hum with energy. The air was thick with the scent of aged parchment and incense.

She took a tentative step forward, her footsteps echoing softly against the polished stone floor. As she moved deeper into the library, she felt an overwhelming sense of familiarity - as though she had been here before in another life.

"Welcome," a voice said suddenly, soft yet resonant.

Mei Ling turned quickly toward its source and saw a figure emerging from between two towering shelves. He was an elderly man with flowing robes adorned with intricate symbols representing harmony and balance. His face was serene yet commanding, his eyes twinkling with wisdom that seemed to span centuries.

"Who are you?" Mei Ling asked hesitantly.

The man smiled faintly. "I am Laozi," he replied simply. "Your ancestor."

Mei Ling's breath caught in her throat. Laozi — the legendary Taoist philosopher whose teachings had shaped generations — was her ancestor? She had studied his writings extensively during her university years but had never imagined such a connection could exist.

"Why have you brought me here?" she asked after a moment, her voice trembling slightly.

"To remind you," Laozi said gently as he gestured toward the shelves around them. "True strength lies not only in intellect but also within your heart - the ability to harmonize with those around you."

As he spoke, images began to appear before Mei Ling -scenes of great battles where strategy and wisdom triumphed over brute force; moments where compassion mended divisions that seemed insurmountable; instances where balance was restored through careful thought and action.

"You possess great knowledge," Laozi continued, his gaze steady on hers. "But knowledge without wisdom is like a blade without a hilt - dangerous and incomplete."

Mei Ling nodded slowly as his words sank in. She had always prided herself on her intellect, but now she realized there was more to leadership than logic alone.

"What must I do?" she asked earnestly.

Laozi smiled again and extended his hand toward her. In his palm rested a small jade pendant carved into the shape of a yin-yang symbol.

"This is your anchor," he said softly. "It will remind you of your purpose when doubt clouds your mind."

Mei Ling reached out hesitantly and took the pendant from his hand. As soon as her fingers closed around it, she felt a warmth spread through her chest - a sense of clarity and peace unlike anything she had ever experienced before.

"Thank you," she whispered, tears welling in her eyes.

Laozi inclined his head slightly but said nothing more as he began to fade from view along with the library around them.

When Mei Ling opened her eyes again, she was back by the fire surrounded by Jelani, Kofi, and Amara. She blinked rapidly as though trying to adjust to reality after what felt like an eternity in another world.

"What did you see?" Jelani asked gently.

Mei Ling smiled faintly as she held up the jade pendant that now rested in her palm - a tangible reminder of her journey.

"I met Laozi," she said softly. "He taught me about balance… about finding harmony between knowledge and wisdom."

Jelani nodded approvingly while Kofi watched silently, his expression unreadable.

"It's your turn now," Mei Ling said after a moment, turning toward him with an encouraging smile.

Kofi hesitated briefly before nodding resolutely. He rose to his feet and stepped into the center of the circle where Amara had already begun preparing for his rite.

"Close your eyes," Amara instructed once more as she resumed chanting in that ancient language that seemed to resonate deep within their souls.

Kofi complied reluctantly at first but soon found himself sinking into a trance-like state similar to what Jelani and Mei Ling had experienced earlier.

In his vision, Kofi found himself standing in a dense forest surrounded by towering trees whose branches intertwined overhead like an intricate web. The air was thick with moisture and filled with the sounds of rustling leaves and distant bird calls.

He looked down at his hands and saw that they were roughened from years of labor - calloused yet strong. In one hand he held a hammer; in the other, a piece of raw iron waiting to be shaped into something useful.

"You have been given great gifts," a voice said suddenly from behind him - a voice that was both gentle and commanding at once.

Kofi turned quickly to see a woman approaching him through the trees. She was tall and regal with dark skin that seemed to glow faintly in the dappled sunlight filtering through the canopy above them. Her clothing was adorned with vibrant patterns reminiscent of traditional Mali designs.

"Who are you?" Kofi asked cautiously.

"I am Amina," she replied simply but with an air of authority that left no room for doubt. "Your ancestor."

Kofi's heart swelled at her words; he had always felt a deep connection to his heritage but had never imagined meeting someone who embodied it so fully.

"What do you want from me?" he asked after a moment's pause.

Amina smiled faintly as she gestured toward an anvil that had appeared nearby along with a roaring forge that filled the air with heat and light.

"To remind you," she said firmly as she placed a piece of raw iron on the anvil before handing him his hammer once more. "Strength comes not only from forging weapons but also from nurturing relationships among those who walk beside us."

Kofi hesitated briefly before stepping forward toward the forge, where sparks danced like fireflies against the twilight sky. All around him, the crowd watched intently - waiting patiently, hoping desperately to find the answers they needed.

They longed for guidance, for a sign to illuminate the path ahead, leading them toward a brighter future. Their eyes remained fixed on the moment, their breaths held in silent anticipation. The air was thick with unspoken prayers, each heart yearning for direction.

And so, with steady resolve, Kofi took another step forward.

CHAPTER 5

THE JOURNEY BEGINS

The dawn broke over the prehistoric landscape, casting a golden hue across the valley. Jelani awoke to the sound of birds chirping and the distant rustle of leaves swaying in the morning breeze. He sat up slowly, still feeling the lingering energy from his encounter with Shaka Zulu. The memories of their shared strength and purpose filled him with resolve.

As he stretched and took in his surroundings, he noticed Mei Ling already awake, her gaze fixed on the horizon. She was deep in thought, her brow furrowed as if contemplating the weight of their newfound responsibilities.

"Good morning," Jelani said, breaking the silence.

Mei Ling turned to him, a smile breaking through her contemplative expression. "Good morning. I was just thinking about what we learned during the rites. We have so much to do."

Jelani nodded, feeling a sense of urgency swell within him. "We need to find out more about this Shadow Wraith and how it connects to our ancestors. Amara mentioned that many have been drawn here—perhaps we can seek them out."

Just then, Kofi emerged from his makeshift shelter, rubbing sleep from his eyes. "What's this about a shadow? Did I miss something?"

Jelani and Mei Ling exchanged glances before Jelani recounted their experiences from the night before—how they had each connected with their ancestors and learned about their strengths.

Kofi listened intently, his expression shifting from confusion to intrigue. "So we're not just here to survive; we're meant to confront this darkness together?"

"Exactly," Mei Ling replied, her voice filled with determination. "But we need more information. If others have been brought here as well, they might know something we don't."

"Let's gather our supplies and head toward that ridge we saw last night," Jelani suggested, pointing toward a distant rise where trees thinned out into open ground. "We can get a better view of the valley from there."

The trio quickly packed their belongings and set off toward the ridge, their hearts pounding with anticipation for what lay ahead. As they climbed higher, the landscape unfolded before them like a vibrant tapestry—lush greens interspersed with patches of golden grass and winding streams that sparkled in the sunlight.

When they reached the top, they paused to catch their breath and take in the breathtaking view. The valley stretched out below them, dotted with small clusters of trees and signs of life—a distant plume of smoke rose into the sky.

"Look!" Kofi exclaimed, pointing toward a clearing where several figures were gathered around a fire pit. "It seems like there are others down there."

Jelani squinted against the sunlight. "We should approach cautiously. We don't know if they're friendly."

As they made their way down the ridge, Jelani felt a mix of excitement and trepidation. The closer they got to the gathering, the more he could hear snippets of conversation—laughter mingled with serious discussions that hinted at shared struggles.

When they reached the edge of the clearing, they paused behind a cluster of trees to observe. A diverse group was gathered around the fire—men and women dressed in various styles reminiscent of ancient cultures from both Africa and Asia. Their faces were animated as they exchanged stories and shared food.

"Should we introduce ourselves?" Mei Ling whispered.

"Let's wait a moment," Jelani replied quietly. "We need to assess whether they pose a threat first."

As they watched, one figure stood out among the rest—a tall woman with striking features adorned in intricate beadwork that shimmered in the sunlight. She commanded attention as she spoke passionately to those around her.

"I tell you all," she declared loudly, "the Shadow Wraith is not just a myth! It has been stalking us for too long! We must unite our strength if we are to stand against it!"

Jelani exchanged glances with Mei Ling and Kofi; this was exactly what they needed to hear. They stepped forward cautiously until they were within earshot.

"Excuse us!" Jelani called out as he approached the group, raising his hands in peace. "We mean no harm! We've come seeking information about this Shadow Wraith."

The woman turned sharply at his voice, her expression shifting from surprise to curiosity. "And who are you?" she asked, her tone demanding yet intrigued.

"I'm Jelani," he replied confidently, gesturing to Mei Ling and Kofi beside him. "These are my companions - Mei Ling and Kofi. We've recently arrived in this land and have heard tales of an ancient evil threatening our existence."

The woman studied them for a moment before nodding slowly. "I am Nyala," she said finally. "Leader of this gathering." She gestured for them to join her circle around the fire.

As they settled in among Nyala's group, Jelani felt an immediate sense of camaraderie - a shared understanding that transcended words.

"We've faced challenges since arriving here," Nyala continued after introducing them to others in her group - a mix of warriors and scholars who had also been drawn into this world by forces beyond their comprehension.

"What do you know about this Shadow Wraith?" Kofi asked directly.

Nyala's expression grew serious as she leaned closer to them all gathered around fire pit flickering brightly illuminating faces surrounding it casting shadows dancing across ground beneath feet planted firmly upon soil nourishing life all around them too!

"It is said that it feeds on fear," Nyala explained gravely. "It twists reality itself - creating illusions that prey upon our deepest insecurities."

Jelani felt a chill run down his spine at her words - a reminder that darkness could manifest not only as physical threats but also psychological ones designed break spirits weaken resolve!

"We've already encountered some manifestations of its power," Mei Ling added thoughtfully.

"During our rites last night... it felt like something was watching us."

CHAPTER 6

SHADOWS UNVEILED

The sun hung low in the sky as Nyala continued sharing stories about encounters with the Shadow Wraith - each tale more chilling than the last. The air around them grew heavy with tension as shadows lengthened across the clearing. The flickering fire cast dancing silhouettes on the faces of those gathered, each expression reflecting a mix of fear and determination.

"It is said that it feeds on fear," Nyala explained gravely, her voice steady yet laced with urgency. "It twists reality itself - creating illusions that prey upon our deepest insecurities."

Jelani felt a chill run down his spine at her words - a reminder that darkness could manifest not only as physical threats but also psychological ones designed to break spirits and weaken resolve.

"We've already encountered some manifestations of its power," Mei Ling added thoughtfully, her brow furrowed in concentration. "During our rites last night… it felt like something was watching us."

Nyala nodded knowingly; her eyes lit up with understanding as she glanced around at the others present - all listening intently, absorbing every word spoken aloud. The crackling fire illuminated their faces, revealing a mixture of hope and trepidation.

"What can we do?" Kofi asked urgently. "How can we fight back against something so insidious?"

Nyala leaned forward, her voice steady yet filled with urgency. "We must unite our strengths - the skills each one possesses can create a force strong enough to repel this darkness."

Jelani felt a surge of determination at her words; he knew that together they could forge an alliance capable of facing whatever lay ahead. "We have ancestral connections," he said passionately. "Our ancestors have bestowed upon us unique gifts - strengths that can help us combat this evil!"

Nyala nodded appreciatively at his fervor while glancing around at the others gathered closely listening intently. "Then let us train together," she proposed after considering their words carefully. "We will prepare ourselves for battle against this darkness!"

The group erupted into murmurs of agreement; excitement rippled through those gathered as hope ignited within hearts yearning to break free from the chains binding them tightly together.

As night fell over the valley, enveloping everything beneath a blanket of stars twinkling above, a sense of camaraderie blossomed among all present. They shared stories of their pasts - tales of bravery and resilience that forged bonds stronger than steel tempered by fires of adversity faced along the way.

Jelani took a moment to observe his companions - their faces illuminated by the firelight, each one reflecting a unique blend of strength and vulnerability. He felt grateful for their presence, realizing how far they had come together in such a short time.

"Tomorrow we will begin our training," Nyala announced, her voice cutting through the chatter like a knife. "We will focus on honing our abilities and learning to trust one another fully."

As they settled into their makeshift camp for the night, Jelani found himself lying awake, staring up at the stars scattered across the vast expanse above. He thought about

Shaka Zulu's words - the importance of courage and wisdom - and how they would need both to face the challenges ahead.

The following days were filled with rigorous training sessions led by Nyala; she taught them how to harness their ancestral abilities while emphasizing the importance of teamwork and collaboration among all present. They practiced combat techniques under her watchful eye, learning to move as one cohesive unit rather than individual warriors.

"Focus on your breathing," Nyala instructed during one session as they stood in a circle, each person preparing to demonstrate their skills. "Let your instincts guide you."

Jelani felt adrenaline coursing through his veins as he prepared to showcase his tracking skills. He closed his eyes momentarily, centering himself before stepping forward into the center of the circle.

"Today, I will show you how to read the signs left behind by those who came before us," he said confidently, gesturing toward the ground where faint impressions marked the earth.

He knelt down and pointed out subtle disturbances in the soil - broken twigs, displaced leaves - that told a story only he could decipher. The others watched intently as he explained how these clues revealed not only the presence of animals but also potential dangers lurking nearby.

"Every creature leaves its mark," Jelani continued passionately. "By understanding these signs, we can navigate this world more safely."

Kofi stepped forward next, eager to demonstrate his forging skills. He had spent hours crafting weapons using ancient methods learned from his ancestors - tools imbued with purpose reflecting strength and resilience forged through trials faced together alongside newfound friends united against a common enemy looming ever closer.

"I've made these for us," Kofi announced proudly as he unveiled several beautifully crafted spears adorned with intricate designs that told stories of their heritage. "Each one is unique - just like us."

Mei Ling stepped up next, her confidence growing with each passing day. She began outlining strategies for their training sessions based on what she had learned from Laozi about balance and harmony.

"We need to work together," she emphasized passionately while drawing diagrams in the dirt with a stick. "If we coordinate our efforts effectively - combining our strengths - we can overcome any challenge."

As training progressed over several days - tensions began rising within the group; doubts crept into minds questioning whether they were truly ready to confront this Shadow Wraith.

One evening, after a particularly grueling session beneath the starlit sky, Kofi pulled Jelani aside, away from the others. The group sat in hushed anticipation, watching intently, waiting patiently - hoping, desperately, for the answers that would guide their steps forward toward the brighter future that awaited them all.

"Do you really think we can defeat this Shadow Wraith?" Kofi asked quietly concern etched across his face reflecting uncertainty lingering beneath surface confidence displayed outwardly during training sessions held throughout week gone by!

Jelani paused, carefully considering the question, weighing the meaning behind each syllable uttered. The words echoed through the forest around them, as if time itself had momentarily stood still, granting him the space to reflect deeply on the lessons learned that day.

"I believe we can," he replied finally meeting Kofi's gaze firmly holding steady unwaveringly despite doubts creeping ever closer threatening pull away everything cherished most deeply held close inside souls yearning desperately break free chains binding tightly together keeping locked away forever hidden deep inside shadows lurking just beyond reach!

"But what if we fail?" Kofi pressed further anxiety creeping into voice betraying vulnerability hidden beneath surface confidence displayed outwardly during training sessions held throughout week gone by!

"We won't fail," Jelani asserted firmly, drawing strength from the bond forged between them. Standing side by side, they faced a common enemy, looming ever closer, threatening to consume everything they held dear. Yet, deep within their souls, a yearning burned - to break free from the chains that bound them, to escape the shadows that lurked just beyond reach.

As dawn broke once again over the valley, their resolve solidified. United under the stars shining brightly above, they felt a renewed sense of purpose guiding each step they took together. A brighter future awaited them, and everyone gathered felt an intense anticipation, watching closely and hoping to find the answers they needed to navigate the challenges ahead.

The next morning brought renewed energy; they gathered around Nyala as she outlined their plans for confronting the Shadow Wraith. Each member contributed ideas based on their unique skills and experiences.

"Today we will practice not just our physical abilities but also our mental fortitude," Nyala said firmly, her eyes scanning each face in turn. "We must be prepared for anything this darkness throws at us."

As they trained throughout the day—sweat dripping from brows mingling with laughter echoing through forest surrounding them both right now feeling like time itself stood still momentarily allowing space necessary reflect deeply upon lessons learned here today!

They forged deeper connections among themselves; trust blossomed like wildflowers breaking through rocky soil—a testament resilience found even amidst chaos threatening consume everything cherished most deeply held close inside souls yearning desperately break free chains binding tightly together keeping locked away forever hidden deep inside shadows lurking just beyond reach!

By sunset, exhaustion settled over them like a warm blanket - but it was accompanied by an exhilarating sense of accomplishment. They had grown stronger together - not only physically but emotionally too!

As they sat around the fire sharing stories once more — the flickering flames casting playful shadows against trees surrounding clearing — they felt hopeful about what lay ahead!

"Whatever happens next," Jelani said, finally breaking the heavy silence that had settled over the group. They stood close, watching intently, waiting patiently, hoping desperately for the answers that would guide their next steps toward a brighter future.

"We face it together."

A chorus of agreement followed, each voice ringing out, clear and strong, echoing through the forest around them. In that moment, time itself seemed to stand still, granting them the space to reflect deeply on the lessons learned that day.

CHAPTER 7

THE FIRST TRIAL

The sun rose steadily over the valley, casting a warm glow that illuminated the faces of Jelani, Mei Ling, Kofi, and their newfound allies. After several days of training under Nyala's guidance, they gathered around the fire pit once more. Anticipation crackled in the air like the flames before them as Nyala stood at the forefront.

"Today marks the beginning of our first trial," she announced with authority. "To face the Shadow Wraith effectively, we must first confront our own fears. Each of you will undergo a test designed to challenge your resolve and uncover your true strengths."

Jelani felt a flutter in his stomach as he listened intently to Nyala's words. He had grown stronger during their training sessions but knew that facing his fears would be an entirely different challenge.

"What kind of trial?" Kofi asked curiously.

Nyala gestured toward the dense forest surrounding them. "You will enter these woods alone. Each of you will encounter an illusion crafted by forces beyond our control—something that embodies your deepest fear or doubt."

Mei Ling inhaled sharply at this revelation; her eyes widened as she turned toward Jelani and Kofi beside her.

"Alone? What if we don't come back?" she asked anxiously.

Nyala reassured them calmly yet firmly: "You will return unharmed physically but perhaps changed internally by what you experience within those woods."

With determination rising within him, Jelani stepped forward, ready to face whatever lay ahead.

As he entered the shadows cast by the towering trees, the atmosphere shifted dramatically around him! The sounds outside faded away, replaced by an eerie silence enveloping everything like a shroud, thickening the air and creating an unsettling energy that made every rustle seem significant.

Suddenly, a chilling wind swept through the trees, carrying whispers echoing from every direction! Jelani strained to listen closely; the voices grew louder, forming words that sent shivers down his spine.

"Jelani… you are not worthy… you will fail…"

He clenched his fists tightly, forcing himself to move forward despite the fear clawing inside him. Memories flooded back—his childhood spent listening to stories of bravery and honor from his mother's lips, always admiring the strength that strayed from modern distractions.

A figure emerged from behind a tree—a woman whose features were hauntingly familiar, wearing traditional Zulu attire adorned with beads shimmering in the dim light.

"Mother?" Jelani gasped, recognizing the familiar face etched deeply in his memory.

Her expression was filled with sorrow, reflecting deep disappointment as she stepped closer, her eyes mirroring the same feelings.

"You've abandoned your heritage," she said softly, her voice laced with sadness.

"I'm trying!" Jelani protested, desperately wanting to honor his ancestors and prove himself worthy. He stood tall against the illusionary form looming before him, feeling a surge of determination rise within his heart, beating steadily against his chest, echoing rhythmically alongside the pulse coursing through his veins.

In that moment, clarity shifted inside him. He remembered Shaka's words about courage — strength flowing through his veins like fire, igniting within him a fierce resolve to stand tall and confront his fear head-on, refusing to let it define him any longer.

With newfound confidence coursing through his veins, Jelani emerged from the forest into the sunlight once more, greeted warmly by Mei Ling, who was waiting anxiously nearby, concern etched across her features.

"How did it go?" Mei Ling asked breathlessly, her concern evident as she wanted to hear every detail of his journey facing the fears lurking just beyond reach.

"It was challenging," Jelani admitted, catching his breath, his heart still racing as the rhythm coursed through him, alive and invigorated.

Mei Ling nodded knowingly, understanding what lay ahead for each of them. They exchanged glances filled with encouragement, knowing they would support one another no matter the challenges that awaited beyond the shadows.

CHAPTER 8

CONFRONTING SHADOWS

Kofi stepped into the forest, trepidation swirling in his gut like a storm cloud threatening to unleash its fury at any moment. The moment he crossed into the shade cast by the towering trees, an eerie silence enveloped him - a stark contrast to the vibrant sounds of life outside. He took a deep breath and steadied himself against the weight of expectation pressing down on his shoulders; this trial was not just about confronting an illusion—it was about proving himself worthy of standing alongside Jelani and Mei Ling.

As he ventured deeper into the woods, memories began to surface—fragments of his childhood spent in the lively streets of his neighborhood, filled with laughter and camaraderie. But beneath those joyful moments lay shadows of insecurity and doubt that had always lingered in the background.

Suddenly, the forest around him shifted. The air felt thicker, and an unsettling chill crept down his spine. It was as if the trees themselves were watching him, their twisted branches reaching out like skeletal fingers. A sense of foreboding washed over him, and Kofi's heart raced as he pressed onward, trying to shake the feeling.

Out of the misty shadows, a figure stepped forward — a younger version of himself, a boy about ten years old, with wide eyes filled with wonder and fear. The boy looked up at him, the resemblance uncanny.

"Kofi?" the younger version asked hesitantly. "Are you…are you going to leave me too?"

Kofi's breath caught in his throat. He remembered that little boy vividly — the one who had dreamed of greatness, only to be crushed by the weight of expectation: the pressure to excel in school, to be the star athlete, to always outshine his peers.

"I'm not going to leave you," Kofi said softly, feeling a surge of emotion well up inside him. "I'm here now."

"But you always say that," the younger Kofi replied, his voice filled with despair. "You never do anything great, and you never will. You're not strong enough, smart enough, or brave enough!"

The words pierced Kofi's heart like daggers. He had often felt that he was not enough—always falling short of his own expectations and those of others. But in that moment, he realized that this was only an illusion, a manifestation of his past fears.

Taking a deep breath, Kofi stepped forward. "That's not true," he said firmly. "I'm more than just these doubts. I've faced challenges and fears before, and I will continue to do so. I won't let this illusion define me!"

The younger Kofi's eyes widened, and for a moment, the heavy atmosphere lightened. The shadows that enveloped the boy started to dissipate. "You mean it?" he asked, a hint of hope in his voice.

"Yes," Kofi affirmed, feeling a newfound strength surging through him. "I'm strong, and I've learned from my past. I won't abandon you. Instead, I will embrace my fears and become the person I was meant to be."

With those words, the younger Kofi smiled, and with that smile, the haunting image began to fade away, replaced by a radiant light illuminating the forest around him. The air lightened, and the eerie silence transformed into a gentle rustle of leaves, echoing a sense of peace.

Kofi emerged from the dense thicket, stepping back into the sunlight where Jelani and Mei Ling awaited him. He could see the questions in their eyes, the concern etched on their faces.

"How did it go?" Mei Ling asked, her voice filled with interest.

"It was... enlightening," Kofi replied, catching his breath and feeling a weight lifted off his shoulders. "I faced my fears, and they no longer control me."

Jelani nodded in support, their bond growing stronger through shared experiences. "We can face anything together," he said, a newfound confidence radiating from him.

As they stood together under the warm sun, they knew that the trials they had faced were only the beginning. With the support of one another, they could confront anything that lay ahead, be it Shadow Wraiths or the doubts that lurked within. They were ready to forge their paths forward — together.

CHAPTER 9
THE SHADOW'S REACH

Night fell over the valley like a velvet cloak, casting shadows that stretched far and wide across the landscape. Jelani, Mei Ling, Kofi, and their allies gathered around Nyala once more as she began to speak, her voice carrying both urgency and wisdom.

"Tonight marks another step forward in our journey," Nyala said firmly. "We have faced our fears; now it's time to better understand our enemy."

She paused briefly before continuing, "The Shadow Wraith is not just an illusion or a myth—it is a living darkness with roots deep within this land. It feeds on fear and despair, growing stronger with each passing day."

Mei Ling leaned forward intently, listening closely to Nyala's words. "How do we stop it?" she asked directly.

Nyala nodded thoughtfully before responding. "To defeat such an enemy requires understanding its nature—its weaknesses as well as its strengths. We must venture into lands where darkness reigns supreme."

Kofi frowned slightly at her suggestion but remained resolute alongside his companions.

As they prepared for their journey into darker territories, Jelani couldn't shake an unsettling sense of foreboding beneath the outward confidence they had displayed during the training sessions throughout the past week. But he knew they had come too far to turn back now; together they were stronger than ever, forging bonds tempered by the fires of adversity they had faced along the way, shaping destinies unfolding right before their eyes.

With determination burning within their hearts, they set off under the starlit sky, guided by the faint glow emanating from luminescent plants scattered across the landscape—an enchanting phenomenon unique to this mystical world, where ancient magic still lingers. The atmosphere thickened with anticipation as they ventured deeper into the unknown.

As they proceeded, the air grew colder, and darkness seemed to press in closer, threatening to consume everything they cherished and held close to their souls, yearning to break free from the chains binding them tightly within the shadows that lurked just beyond reach.

Suddenly, a cloaked figure emerged from the shadows, moving swiftly with silent footsteps barely making a sound against the ground beneath them.

"Who goes there?" Jelani called out sharply, instinctively reaching for the spear resting beside him, ready to defend his companions standing side by side, united against the common enemy looming ever closer.

The figure halted momentarily, then stepped closer, revealing her features illuminated by the faint moonlight filtering through the canopy above. A young woman dressed in simple robes adorned with intricate patterns stepped forward.

"I am Akira," she introduced herself softly yet firmly, extending her hand in a gesture of peace while maintaining unwavering eye contact throughout their exchange, feeling as though time itself stood still, allowing the space necessary to reflect deeply upon the lessons learned.

"I have been sent to guide you through these treacherous lands," Akira explained further, gesturing toward the winding path leading deeper into the heart of the encroaching darkness, casting long, ominous shadows that danced across the ground around them.

Together, they walked silently, following Akira's lead as she navigated the twists and turns of the path, leading them further into the depths of the unknown, shrouded in mystery, with danger lurking around every corner, threatening to take away everything they held dear.

Akira shared stories about her own experiences facing similar trials—tales filled with bravery and resilience, tested courage, and the limits pushed through the exploration of uncharted realms that called to them.

CHAPTER 10
INTO DARKNESS

As they journeyed deeper into unknown territories, guided by Akira, their senses grew sharper, attuned to the subtle changes in the environment that signaled potential dangers lying ahead—unseen yet strongly felt, like a presence hovering just out of sight, always ready to strike without warning. This left no room for error or hesitation as challenges unfolded rapidly, one after another, pushing their limits and testing their resolve. The bonds formed between them grew stronger, like steel tempered in the fires of adversity, shaping their destinies before their very eyes.

Akira led them through dense forests where twisted, gnarled branches reached skyward like skeletal fingers grasping at the heavens above, casting long, ominous shadows that danced across the ground beneath their feet planted firmly on soil that nourished life all around. The air was heavy with mist, obscuring visibility and making every step feel uncertain, yet somehow exhilarating.

They pushed the boundaries further than they had ever imagined, announcing the arrival of a new era filled with hope and resilience forged through trials overcome and courage tested. As they explored these uncharted realms, the illumination of the path ahead guided every step they took.

Suddenly, a low growl echoed through the mist, sending shivers down their spines and causing their hearts to race, the rhythm echoing alongside the pulse coursing through their veins. Their spirits were invigorated as they drew strength from the connection forged among friends standing side by side, united against a common enemy looming ever closer, threatening to consume everything they cherished.

Akira raised her hand, signaling them to halt while she scanned their surroundings cautiously. Her eyes narrowed slightly as she focused intensely on something only she could see amidst the swirling fog that obscured their view, casting an eerie silence around them like a thick shroud. The atmosphere was charged with anticipation, building steadily around them.

"What is it?" Mei Ling whispered softly, concern etched on her face, reflecting the uncertainty that lingered beneath the confidence she had displayed during the training sessions throughout the past week.

Akira hesitated briefly before responding, her voice barely audible over the distant howling wind and rustling leaves, whispering secrets only known to those who dared to listen carefully. She weighed the meaning behind each syllable spoken aloud, feeling that time itself stood still momentarily, allowing them space to reflect deeply on the lessons learned that day.

"There are creatures here unlike any you've seen," Akira warned gravely, her expression serious and mirroring the gravity of the situation unfolding rapidly.

The need for guidance brought them together in unity, emphasizing the collective effort required to overcome the darkness looming ever closer. This darkness threatened to consume their most cherished hopes and deepest souls, which longed for freedom from the chains that bound them, keeping everything locked away deep inside. Yet there was an eternal promise shining like a beacon of light, piercing the veil of uncertainty and illuminating the darkest corners of their existence. This reminder came in the form of glimmers of hope offering solace, comfort, and reassurance — they were never truly alone, for they stood shoulder to shoulder, bound by a shared purpose.

Driven by conviction, they would forge new paths, blaze trails, and chart courses to navigate unmapped waters. They would sail across unknown seas and explore the mysteries of the cosmos, unraveling the enigmas of the past, unlocking doors of perception, and expanding their horizons. They would push frontiers and stretch their imaginations to soar to heights previously unimaginable, like eagles with wings spread wide, embracing the vast expanse of limitless possibilities within them.

Together, they would summon their innermost depths, unleash their inner fire, and ignite their passion. They would fuel their dreams and propel themselves on a trajectory toward infinity, touching the stars. The celestial music of their harmony would create a symphony of creation, vibrating with the frequency and resonance of their heartbeat — a cosmic dance in rhythmic motion, flowing like tides and crashing waves upon shifting shores. As the sands drifted and the winds whispered ancient secrets, they would hear echoes of timeless truths reverberating throughout eternity, filling them with a sense of reverence, gratitude, and compassion for the world around them.

CHAPTER 11

THE HEART OF DARKNESS

As they stood against the pack emerging from the mist, Jelani, Mei Ling, Kofi, and Akira formed a tight circle, ready to face whatever dangers lay ahead. The air was thick with tension, and their hearts pounded in unison as they prepared for battle.

"Stay close," Akira warned softly, her voice barely audible over the distant howling wind and rustling leaves, which whispered secrets only known to those who dared listen carefully. They weighed the meaning behind each syllable, feeling as if time itself stood still momentarily, allowing them the space to reflect deeply upon the lessons learned here today.

The beasts charged forward, their massive bodies hurtling toward the group with an unwavering commitment to protect one another, no matter the odds stacked against them. Survival hung precariously in the balance, as fate decided the course of destiny that would unfold in the next chapter of their saga.

With their spears at the ready, Jelani took the lead position, his movements swift and decisive. He drew strength from the connection forged with his friends, standing side by side united against a common enemy looming ever closer, threatening to consume everything they cherished and held most deeply in their souls.

Mei Ling positioned herself beside him, her strategic mind racing as she devised a plan to fend off the beasts effectively, while also showing empathy toward any potential victims among them. It was a delicate balance between logic and compassion that defined her character, forging bonds stronger than steel, tempered in the fires of adversity faced together, shaping the destinies unfolding right before their eyes.

Kofi stood firm, his hammer at the ready and muscles tensed, preparing to strike down any beast that dared approach too closely. His resilience reflected the trials he had overcome, with courage testing the limits pushed and boundaries explored in uncharted realms.

Akira moved swiftly, her footsteps silent against the ground beneath her feet, firmly planted upon soil nourishing the life surrounding them. Her agility allowed her to dodge attacks with ease, striking back whenever an opportunity arose—a testament to the strength and resilience found even amidst the chaos that threatened to consume everything they cherished.

As the battle raged on, the group began to tire, exhaustion creeping into their limbs and heavy breathing echoing through the thickening atmosphere charged with anticipation. But they refused to give up, drawing strength from their unity—a theme that resonated strongly, emphasizing their collective effort to overcome the darkness looming ever closer.

In their deepest souls, they longed for freedom, breaking the shackles that bound them tightly. They held fast to the eternal promise of a shining beacon of light, piercing through the veil of uncertainty, illuminating the darkest corners of existence. Even in the bleakest moments, there was always a glimmer of light offering solace, comfort, and reassurance that they were never truly alone; they stood shoulder to shoulder, united by a shared purpose and driven by conviction to forge new paths.

A sudden figure emerged from the mist, cloaked and hooded, moving swiftly with silent footsteps that barely made a sound against the ground beneath them.

"Wait!" the figure shouted loudly, their voice carrying across the battlefield and halting the action momentarily as the group turned toward the newcomer, wondering what role they would play in the unfolding drama.

CHAPTER 12

UNEXPECTED ALLIES

The figure stepped closer, revealing a young woman with striking silver hair that framed her determined face. Her piercing green eyes surveyed the group, a mix of concern and resolve evident in her expression.

"I know you," Jelani exclaimed, recognition dawning on him. "You're Lira, the one who travels between the realms!"

Lira nodded, her gaze shifting to the beasts charging from the mist, their growls growing louder. "There's no time for explanations now," she said urgently. "I sensed the disturbance in the balance, and I came to help. These creatures are drawn to your energy. We need to fend them off together."

Mei Ling's eyes widened in surprise but quickly regained her composure. "How do we trust you? We don't know your intentions," she replied, gripping her spear tighter.

Lira held up her hands in a gesture of peace. "I understand your hesitation. But I'm here to stop the impending darkness, just like you. We share the same goal. Let me show you."

As they spoke, the pack of beasts closed in, their eyes glinting with a predatory hunger. With a swift motion, Lira raised her hands, and a shimmering barrier of light surged forth, pushing back the nearest creatures. The air crackled with energy, forming a protective cocoon around the group.

"We can't hold up the barrier forever. We need to fight back," Kofi shouted, rallying his friends. He swung his hammer, aiming at the nearest beast, and with a mighty strike, he sent it crashing to the ground.

Emboldened by Kofi's strength, Akira and Jelani moved in sync, attacking alongside Lira's barrier. "Focus on the ones attacking from the sides!" Akira called out, her movements fluid as she deflected a beast's strike with her spear.

The group worked as a well-oiled machine, their trust in one another growing with each passing moment. Lira showed them how to channel their energy into their strikes, amplifying their power and granting them newfound agility.

Amidst the fray, Mei Ling's calm presence shone through. "Remember why we fight!" she shouted, her voice cutting through the chaos. "For those we love and the future we seek!"

Each of them, reinvigorated by her words, pushed against the tide of beasts. They fought not just for survival but for the promise of hope that flickered in their hearts. The battle was fierce, but with Lira's assistance, they began to gain the upper hand.

As they took down the last of the charging beasts, a sudden silence fell over the battlefield. Breathing heavily, the group glanced around at the aftermath—

a mixture of panting breaths and the echo of their hearts reverberated in the stillness.

Lira let out a long sigh, her shoulders relaxing for the first time since her arrival. "You fought bravely. I can sense you've all been through much together. The darkness is strong, but so is your resolve."

Jelani looked at her, curiosity piqued. "Why do you care? What's your stake in all this?"

Lira stepped closer, her expression earnest. "I have witnessed the devastation caused by this darkness across realms. Each battle fought here sends ripples through the fabric of reality, impacting lives beyond your own. I cannot stand by while such devastation occurs. We are bound by fate now, all of us."

Kofi rubbed the back of his neck, his brow furrowed. "Alright, we'll take your help—but if you try anything, we will be ready."

Lira nodded, understanding their caution. "Trust will take time, but together, we can push back the darkness."

As they caught their breath, the sun began to rise, casting golden rays through the mist. It felt as if a new beginning was dawning, a promise of light to guide them further into the unknown.

"Let us move forward," Akira suggested, her spirit renewed. "We have much to uncover and more battles to face."

With Lira now among them, the group set off, determined to unravel the mysteries ahead and confront the threats that loomed on the horizon. Little did they know that the journey would test their bonds in ways they could never imagine, forging alliances that would shape their destinies.

CHAPTER 13

THE ANCIENT RUINS

As they ventured deeper into the ancient ruins, Zarek led them through winding paths lined with crumbling stone walls adorned with intricate carvings. These carvings reflected stories of forgotten civilizations that once flourished here, leaving behind remnants of a legacy that shaped the world today. The bonds formed among them were stronger than steel, tempered by the fires of adversity they faced, shaping destinies that unfolded right before their eyes. They watched intently, waiting patiently, hoping desperately to find the answers needed to guide their steps toward a brighter future.

The air was filled with an eerie silence, punctuated only by the distant howling wind and the rustling leaves that seemed to whisper secrets known only to those who dared listen carefully. It felt as if time itself stood still, allowing them the space to reflect deeply on the lessons learned that day.

Jelani couldn't help but feel a sense of awe at the sheer scale and craftsmanship evident in these structures—a testament to the strength and resilience found even amidst chaos, which threatened to consume everything they cherished. They held these memories dear, yearning to break free from the chains that bound them tightly, kept locked away within the shadows lurking just beyond reach.

Mei Ling moved cautiously, her strategic mind racing as she devised a plan to navigate the labyrinthine passages. At the same time, she showed empathy towards any potential victims among them—a delicate balance between logic and compassion that defined her character. The bonds they formed were stronger than steel, tempered by the fires of adversity they faced, shaping destinies unfolding right before their eyes.

Kofi stood firm, his hammer at the ready, muscles tensed as he prepared to strike down any danger that dared approach too closely. His resilience was forged in the trials he had overcome, with courage tested and limits pushed, exploring uncharted realms that beckoned discovery, illuminating the path ahead and guiding every step.

Akira moved swiftly, her footsteps barely making a sound against the ground beneath her feet. Her agility allowed her to dodge attacks with ease, striking back whenever an opportunity arose. She embodied the strength and resilience found even amidst chaos, yearning to break free from the chains that bound her tightly.

As they explored further, they stumbled upon a large chamber filled with ancient artifacts—relics of past civilizations that told stories of forgotten wisdom echoing through the ages. These artifacts resonated deeply within their hearts, beating steadily against their chests, echoing rhythmically alongside the pulses coursing through their veins, invigorating their spirits and guiding every decision made together as friends united against a common enemy looming ever closer.

Suddenly, a faint glow emanated from the center of the room, illuminating the dusty relics and casting long, ominous shadows that danced across the ground beneath their feet.

Zarek approached cautiously, his eyes narrowing as he focused intensely on something only he could see amidst the swirling fog and eerie silence, which enveloped everything like a thick shroud. Anticipation built steadily around them.

"What is it?" Mei Ling whispered softly, concern etched on her face, reflecting the uncertainty that lay beneath the confidence she displayed during the training sessions that had taken place throughout the past week.

Zarek hesitated briefly before responding in a quiet voice, barely audible over the distant howling wind and the rustling leaves that whispered secrets for those willing to listen. "There's a prophecy etched into this artifact," he explained, gesturing toward the glowing relic that radiated light, illuminating the darkness and pushing back the shadows lurking just beyond their reach.

He reminded them of why they had come together, forging bonds stronger than steel, tempered by the fires of adversity they faced along the way, shaping destinies that unfolded right before their eyes. "We are strongest together," he said, emphasizing the theme of unity that resonated deeply among them.

CHAPTER 14

THE PROPHECY UNVEILED

As Zarek spoke about the prophecy etched into the artifact, the group leaned in closer, their expressions a mix of fascination and apprehension. A faint glow emanated from the relic, casting long, ominous shadows that danced across the ground beneath their feet—solidly planted on the earth that nourished the thriving life all around them. The air grew heavier with each word Zarek articulated, thick with anticipation. His presence seemed to draw them deeper into the depths of an ancient mystery, an intimacy that made them feel both vulnerable and empowered.

Zarek began to translate the ancient text inscribed on the surface of the relic, his voice steady yet laced with urgency. The gravity of the situation unfolded rapidly, layer by layer, revealing truths long buried in time. "This is not merely a tale," he emphasized, "but a foretelling of events yet to come. We stand on the precipice of destiny, and it is our actions that will shape the outcome."

One challenge after another had pushed their limits, testing their resolve and forging bonds that were stronger than steel, tempered in the fires of adversity. As the narrative unfolded, destinies intertwined right before their watchful eyes. Each member of the group felt the weight of the unfolding saga. They absorbed Zarek's words, feeling their hearts beat in sync, waiting with an intense, hopeful intent, desperate for guidance, as they moved toward the better futures that awaited them.

The theme of unity resonated strongly in Zarek's translation, emphasizing the collective effort required to overcome the encroaching darkness. This dark force was not merely an external threat but also a consuming shadow lurking in their deepest souls, longing for freedom, their very being shackled by circumstances beyond their control.

An eternal promise shone like a beacon of light in Zarek's narrative, piercing the veil of uncertainty and illuminating the darkest corners of their existence. It served as a reminder that even in the bleakest moments—when hope seemed like a distant memory—there was always a glimmer of light offering solace, comfort, and reassurance.

"You are never truly alone," Zarek declared, his voice rising above the whispers of the wind. "You stand shoulder to shoulder, bound not only by fate but also by a shared purpose and driven by unwavering conviction. Together, you are strong enough to face any storm."

With newfound determination, the group recognized that they were destined to forge new paths, blaze trails, and chart courses into the unknown. They were set to navigate uncharted waters and sail seas filled with uncertainty but also with untold wonders. They would unlock the mysteries of the cosmos and unravel the enigmas of the past that had long since been forgotten, expanding their perceptions and pushing the frontiers of imagination further than anyone had ever dared to dream.

Jelani felt a surge of determination rise within him. He recognized himself as the earth warrior—strong and resilient, he embodied a solid foundation for the group, steadfast in the face of challenges. "I will be your shield," he declared, his voice steady. "I will stand tall against the forces that seek to destroy the balance of nature and protect the harmony among the elements that are essential to our survival."

The weight of Jelani's words lingered in the air, resonating deeply in the hearts of his companions. He knew that nurturing growth and renewal cycles were vital for sustaining life, enabling their inherent freedoms. He envisioned himself as a guardian of the land, ensuring that the life force flowed freely, unencumbered by external threats that sought to disrupt the natural order.

Mei Ling nodded in understanding, recognizing herself as the water warrior—a fluid, adaptable, yet powerful force capable of great healing. "Water is both gentle and fierce," she explained, her voice flowing like a calm stream. "I will soothe the wounds inflicted upon others while also possessing the strength to protect my allies. No matter how high the odds are stacked against us, I am committed to safeguarding our collective existence."

Her declaration mirrored the flow of a vast river, a balance of strength and serenity, and it carried a promise to support the group through turbulent times. With her capacity to heal and adapt, she embraced her role, ready to act as the calming force whenever tumult threatened their journey.

Kofi stepped forward confidently, acknowledging his identity as the fire warrior—a passionate protector driven by a burning desire to defend his loved ones. "Fire represents transformation," he proclaimed, a fierce light sparking in his eyes. "Through my flames, I will forge weapons to protect those I care for, not for personal glory or recognition, but as a testament to resilience forged from trials overcome."

He spoke with the intensity of a blazing hearth, warmth encircling the group and igniting their spirits. His determination was rooted in a profound desire to rise above challenges, and his courage would illuminate their path even in the darkest nights.

Akira smiled softly, embracing her role as the air warrior—agile and swift, she stepped lightly as if floating on unseen currents. "I will be the messenger connecting worlds," she said, her voice airy yet filled with importance. "Like the wind, I will bridge gaps between realms, drawing forth the lessons of the past to inform our present and future."

Her words danced in the air, weaving an intricate tapestry of connection. She understood the unseen forces influencing their lives, the energies that shaped their destiny: "I will navigate the currents of fate, helping us all remain mindful of the lessons learned by those who walked before us, ensuring we do not repeat their mistakes."

As they gathered together, their hearts intertwined through a spirit of camaraderie, they recognized the strength they held as one. The air shimmered with an electric energy, their resolve fortified, as they grasped the truth of Zarek's prophecy: they were indeed strongest together. The theme of unity would guide them through perilous times, and they felt the collective heartbeat of their aspirations reverberate within them, a rhythmic pulse igniting courage in their hearts as they faced the darkness threatening their realm.

Zarek's voice rose, encapsulating the essence of their journey. "Do not fear the shadows," he said, "but embrace the light that shines within each of you. Let it illuminate your paths ahead. You are chosen for this task, not by chance, but by fate. The power you possess is not merely a birthright; it is a legacy awaiting your claim."

With every word, the vision of their quest solidified, a tapestry woven from aspirations and destinies. They each took a moment to reflect on their paths, the sacrifices made, and the experiences that carved them into who they were.

They would challenge the Shadow Wraith's power with all their might, wielding their elemental gifts as weapons against the encroaching darkness.

United by purpose and strengthened by their shared convictions, the four warriors prepared to embark on their journey. They stood together, ready to embrace the challenges ahead, fueled by the promise of unity. Each was a vital thread in the fabric of their collective destiny, intertwined in a saga that would reverberate through the ages, echoing tales of bravery, resilience, and hope.

As the light of the relic flickered and dimmed, each warrior felt a new flame of determination igniting within them. They were ready to unlock the gateways of their potential, exploring the realms that lay ahead, not just as individuals but as a cohesive force—one that would transcend the boundaries of time and space, united in their quest to reclaim balance and restore harmony to their world. Their journey was just beginning, and every step they took would lead them closer to fulfilling the prophecy and shaping a future illuminated by hope.

CHAPTER 15

TRIALS OF WATER

The air crackled with energy as Kofi stepped into the fiery chamber, flames twisting and writhing like wild spirits. Heat radiated from every corner, not just from the molten walls and searing ground, but from something deeper—an ancient, pulsing force that seemed to beckon him forward. This was more than just a test of endurance; it was a trial of his very essence.

"Remember your purpose," Zarek's voice echoed in his mind. "You must confront your fears to unlock your true potential."

Kofi inhaled deeply, grounding himself amidst the flickering chaos. His heart pounded, not from fear, but from the sheer weight of the moment. He had trained for this, fought for this, and now the flames themselves demanded proof of his strength.

"I am more than my doubts," he whispered, recalling the encouragement of his friends. "I am fire."

Suddenly, the inferno shifted. A towering figure emerged from the depths of the flames, its form massive and imposing. It was forged entirely from molten rock, its eyes burning like twin suns. Lava dripped from its body, sizzling upon contact with the scorched earth. The ground trembled beneath its steps.

"What do you seek, Fire Warrior?" The beast's voice was like distant thunder, rumbling through the chamber.

"I seek strength!" Kofi shouted, his stance unyielding. "Strength to protect my friends and my home!"

The creature let out a guttural laugh, the sound reverberating through the walls. "Strength? You think you possess it? Show me!"

With those words, the chamber erupted in a storm of flames, and the beast lunged forward, swinging a massive, molten fist. Kofi barely had time to react. He dodged, rolling to the side as the ground where he had stood moments ago exploded in a burst of fire and molten rock. The heat was suffocating, but he pushed through, gripping his hammer tightly.

He counterattacked, swinging his weapon with all his might. The hammer struck the beast's arm, but instead of causing damage, it barely made an impact.

The creature's molten form absorbed the blow, the lava shifting and reforming seamlessly.

"Is that all you have?" the beast taunted. "Brute force alone will not defeat me."

Kofi clenched his jaw, frustration simmering within him. He thought back to his training — the lessons from Jelani about grounding himself like earth, from Mei Ling about fluidity, from Akira about agility. He needed more than raw power. He needed balance.

He took a steadying breath, adjusting his stance. Fire wasn't just destruction — it was transformation. Creation. He closed his eyes for a fraction of a second, feeling the energy around him, the heat pulsing in sync with his own heartbeat. When he opened them, clarity replaced frustration.

"Focus." He exhaled, centering himself.

The beast roared again, hurling another wave of fire. This time, Kofi didn't dodge. Instead, he embraced the flames, drawing them in, letting them swirl around him. The inferno bent to his will, the fire becoming an extension of himself. He was no longer merely resisting the heat — he was a part of it.

With renewed confidence, he surged forward. His movements were different now — not just powerful, but precise. He dodged with fluidity, striking where the creature was most vulnerable. He saw the subtle shifts in its molten armor, the moments where the lava cooled just slightly before reheating. Those were his targets.

He attacked again, this time aiming for those weak points. His hammer, now ablaze with the same fire that surrounded him, struck true. The beast stumbled, letting out a roar that was equal parts anger and surprise.

"You think fire alone will save you?" it snarled.

"I don't just wield fire," Kofi growled, his eyes blazing

The battle intensified. The chamber became a whirlwind of heat and embers, the two combatants locked in a dance of power and resilience. Kofi moved with newfound agility, his strikes landing with increasing force. Each hit sent cracks spider-webbing across the creature's form, molten chunks breaking away.

The beast, sensing its weakening state, let out a final, desperate attack. It summoned all its remaining energy, forming a massive firestorm, a swirling vortex of flames meant to consume everything in its path.

Kofi didn't hesitate. He planted his feet firmly, raising his hammer high. Drawing upon every ounce of strength, every lesson, every moment that had led him here, he channeled the fire within. With one final, devastating strike, he brought his hammer down, splitting the inferno apart.

The impact sent a shockwave through the chamber. The beast let out a deafening roar as its molten form shattered, dissolving into embers and ash. The storm faded, the flames dimming until only a soft glow remained.

Panting, Kofi stood amidst the remnants of battle, exhilarated yet humbled. He had won.

"You have proven yourself," Zarek's voice resonated in his mind. "But remember — this is only one trial."

As the last embers faded into the darkness, Kofi turned toward the archway ahead. Beyond the ruins, deeper in the shadows, the next challenge awaited.

And he was ready.

CHAPTER 16

TRIALS OF FIRE

Mei Ling stood at the edge of an expansive chamber, her breath catching as she took in the sight before her. A vast lake stretched out before her, its surface shimmering under an ethereal light that seemed to come from nowhere yet everywhere at once. The air was cool and crisp, carrying the faint scent of water and stone. Gentle waves lapped against the chamber's walls, creating a rhythmic sound that both soothed and unsettled her.

"This is my trial," she whispered to herself, her voice barely audible over the soft ripples of the water. "I must embrace my element."

She took a deep breath, closing her eyes for a moment to center herself. The lessons from her training echoed in her mind—adaptability, fluidity, and balance. She had always been the strategist, the planner, but this trial demanded something more. It required her to let go of control and trust in the unknown.

"Be like water," she murmured, recalling Nyala's words. "Strong enough to carve stone but gentle enough to nurture life."

As if in response to her resolve, the water began to stir. Ripples spread across the surface, growing larger and more erratic. Suddenly, a figure emerged from beneath the lake—a being of pure water with flowing hair like liquid silver and eyes as deep as the ocean.

"What do you seek, water warrior?" it asked, its voice resonating through the chamber like a melody carried on waves.

Mei Ling straightened her posture and met the spirit's gaze with unwavering determination. "I seek adaptability," she replied firmly. "I want to learn how to flow with challenges rather than resist them."

The spirit tilted its head, studying her intently. "To adapt is to flow like water—ever-changing yet constant in purpose," it said softly. "But adaptability comes at a price. You must face your fears and surrender your need for control."

Before Mei Ling could respond, the spirit raised its hand. The calm waters erupted into chaos as powerful currents surged around her feet. Without hesitation, she stepped into the lake, allowing herself to be pulled into its depths.

The world shifted as she submerged beneath the surface. The light above faded into darkness, replaced by an otherworldly glow emanating from within the water itself. Swirling currents surrounded her, tugging at her body in every direction. It was disorienting and overwhelming—a test of both her physical strength and mental focus.

"Stay calm," she reminded herself, inhaling deeply through her nose despite being underwater. She focused on steadying her thoughts and letting go of resistance. Instead of fighting against the currents, she allowed them to guide her.

Suddenly, a shadow emerged from the depths—a monstrous creature formed from swirling water and darkness. Its eyes glowed with malice as it moved toward her with predatory intent.

"What do you want?" Mei Ling shouted into the void, her voice carrying effortlessly through the water.

"I want to see if you can truly adapt," it growled in response. Its voice was deep and guttural, reverberating through the chamber like thunder crashing over waves.

The creature lunged toward her with terrifying speed, its massive form cutting through the water like a blade. Mei Ling reacted instinctively, twisting her body to evade its attack. She moved with precision and grace, weaving through the currents as if they were an extension of herself.

"Use your surroundings," she reminded herself aloud, recalling Nyala's teachings during their training sessions. "Water is not just an obstacle—it's my ally."

As she maneuvered through the depths, Mei Ling began to harness the energy around her. She extended her arms outward, feeling the currents respond to her will. With a flick of her wrist, she sent a wave crashing into the creature's side.

The beast roared in anger but quickly recovered, turning its glowing eyes toward her once more. "You cannot defeat me!" it snarled as it charged again.

Mei Ling narrowed her eyes and steadied herself against the oncoming attack. She realized that brute force alone wouldn't be enough to overcome this foe; she needed to think strategically — to adapt.

"I don't need to defeat you," she said calmly as an idea formed in her mind. "I just need to outlast you."

Instead of attacking head-on, Mei Ling began using the currents to redirect the creature's movements. She led it into whirlpools and eddies that slowed its momentum while conserving her own energy. Each time it lunged at her, she evaded gracefully — flowing like water itself.

The battle continued for what felt like hours until finally, the creature began to falter. Its form grew less defined, as if it were dissolving back into the lake from which it had emerged.

"You have proven yourself," it said reluctantly before disappearing into mist.

The waters calmed around Mei Ling as silence enveloped her once more. She floated for a moment in stillness—her heart pounding but filled with a sense of accomplishment.

When she finally emerged from the lake's surface— her body drenched but her spirit renewed—she found herself standing back at the edge of the chamber where Zar awaited her.

CHAPTER 17

THE GATHERING STORM

The atmosphere in the ancient ruins shifted as Jelani, Kofi, Mei Ling, and Akira regrouped after completing their trials. Each had faced their fears and emerged stronger, but a sense of urgency hung in the air. The trials had only been the beginning—a test to prove their worth. Now, a greater challenge loomed ahead, one that would require not only their strength but their unity.

Zarek stood before them, his expression grave, his piercing gaze scanning each of them as though assessing their readiness. His dark robes fluttered slightly in the unnatural wind that swept through the chamber, carrying with it the faint whispers of unseen forces. A heavy silence settled over the group.

"You have proven yourselves as warriors," he began, his voice low and steady, carrying an undeniable weight. "But the Shadow Wraith's power is growing stronger. We must prepare for the challenges ahead."

"What do we need to do?" Kofi asked, his brow furrowing with concern. His fingers tightened around the hilt of his weapon, an unconscious reaction to the mounting tension.

Zarek gestured toward a large stone table at the center of the chamber, covered in maps and ancient texts, their edges frayed with age. "We need to gather information about the Shadow Wraith's movements and its minions. We cannot confront it without understanding its strategies."

Mei Ling stepped closer, her keen eyes scanning the markings on the maps. "These symbols… they indicate areas where darkness has spread," she noted, tracing her finger along a jagged line that cut across the landscape like an ominous scar.

"Yes," Zarek confirmed. "These are places where the Wraith has been active—towns that have fallen into despair, lands swallowed by its influence. We need to visit these locations, rally any survivors, and uncover the Wraith's next move."

Jelani felt a surge of determination, his fists clenching. "We can't let this darkness consume our home. We have to act quickly."

Akira nodded, her usual calm now laced with urgency. "But we must also be cautious. The Wraith's minions are lurking in these areas, ready to strike the moment we make ourselves known."

"Then we'll split into two groups," Zarek suggested. "One group will head to the nearest town marked on this map, while the other will scout ahead for any signs of danger."

"I'll take Kofi and Mei Ling with me," Jelani said decisively. "We'll head to the town and gather as many allies as we can."

"I'll go with Akira," Zarek replied. "We'll scout the surrounding areas and assess any threats before you arrive."

With their plan set, they quickly gathered supplies — weapons, food, and anything else they might need for their journey ahead. The weight of their mission settled heavily on their shoulders as they prepared to leave the safety of the ruins.

As they stepped outside, the landscape before them felt eerily still. A chill ran through the air, sending shivers down Jelani's spine. Dark clouds gathered overhead, swirling like a living entity, casting elongated shadows across the land.

"Let's move," Kofi urged, his voice steady despite the unease hanging over them like a dense fog.

The group set off toward the nearest town, navigating through dense forests and rocky terrain. The sun had begun its descent, casting golden light through the thick canopy, but despite its warmth, Jelani couldn't shake the feeling that they were being watched. The silence around them was unnatural. Even the usual rustling of leaves and chirping of birds had vanished, replaced by an oppressive stillness.

"Stay alert," he murmured, scanning their surroundings. "We can't afford to let our guard down."

Mei Ling nodded, though her hands trembled slightly. "What if we encounter one of those creatures? We're not fully prepared yet."

Kofi placed a reassuring hand on her shoulder. "We've faced our fears already," he reminded her. "We can handle whatever comes our way."

As they pressed on, they stumbled upon a clearing where remnants of an old village lay scattered across the ground—crumbling buildings overtaken by creeping vines, shattered windows reflecting the dying light, and eerie silence filling the spaces where life once thrived.

"This must be it," Jelani said quietly as he surveyed the area. "The town is abandoned."

"Wait," Mei Ling whispered, pointing toward a flickering light emanating from one of the dilapidated structures.

Cautiously, they approached the building, weapons drawn and senses heightened. As they entered, they found a small group of survivors huddled around a fire—a mix of weary faces filled with both hope and despair. Their clothes were tattered, their expressions hollow from weeks, perhaps months, of hardship.

"Who are you?" a man asked warily, his voice hoarse from lack of use.

"We're here to help," Jelani replied, lowering his weapon slightly to show he meant no harm. "We're fighting against the Shadow Wraith and its minions."

The survivors exchanged glances before a woman stepped forward, her eyes filled with uncertainty. "You're brave to come here… but what can you do? The darkness has already taken so much from us."

"We can offer you protection," Kofi said earnestly. "But we need your help too—together, we can stand against this evil."

A murmur spread through the group, hesitation warring with a flicker of hope. An older man stepped forward, his face lined with the weight of experience. "I was once a warrior," he admitted. "I fought to protect this village before the Wraith's forces came. But we were outnumbered… We lost so much."

Mei Ling stepped closer. "Then fight with us now. We need people who know these lands, who understand what we're up against."

The old man studied her, then nodded slowly. "If there is still a chance to reclaim what was lost… I will fight."

One by one, others stepped forward, their fear gradually being replaced by resolve. The group that had once been merely survivors was beginning to transform into warriors once more.

Jelani felt a renewed sense of purpose as he listened to their struggles. He knew that together, they could forge an alliance strong enough to stand against whatever lay ahead.

A distant sound echoed through the ruins—low, guttural, inhuman. The Wraith's minions were near.

"Arm yourselves," Jelani said, his voice steady. "The battle begins now."

CHAPTER 18

SHADOWS RISING

Zarek and Akira moved stealthily through the dense forest surrounding the ruins, their senses heightened as they searched for any signs of danger. The oppressive silence weighed heavily on them; every rustle in the underbrush made them pause and listen intently, their hands hovering over their weapons, ready for the slightest threat.

"Do you feel that?" Akira whispered suddenly, her eyes scanning their surroundings. The air was charged, thick with an eerie tension that sent a shiver down her spine.

Zarek nodded grimly. He felt it too—an almost electric energy that signaled something unnatural. "Something is coming," he murmured, gripping his staff tightly.

As if in response to his words, a low, guttural growl echoed through the trees, followed by a series of sharp barks that reverberated through the night like the sound of cracking bones. The chilling noise sent waves of unease rippling through them.

"Stay close," Zarek instructed, his voice barely above a breath. He pulled Akira behind a thick wall of foliage, crouching low as they observed the shifting shadows ahead.

From their vantage point, they spotted a pack of creatures prowling through the woods. Twisted forms, cloaked in darkness itself, moved with an unnatural grace. Their glowing eyes flickered like embers in the night, scanning for prey. Tendrils of shadow curled from their bodies, distorting the air around them.

"What are those things?" Akira asked breathlessly, her heart hammering against her ribs. The sight before her was like something out of a nightmare.

Zarek's expression hardened. "Minions of the Shadow Wraith," he confirmed. "Creatures of darkness, born from its will. If they are here, it means the Wraith's influence is growing stronger."

Akira felt a lump form in her throat. "We need to warn Jelani's group! If these things find them—"

Zarek held up a hand, stopping her. "If we run now, we'll lead them straight to them. We can't risk that."

Akira bit her lip, frustration and fear warring within her. "Then what do we do? We can't just stand here."

Zarek exhaled deeply, weighing their options. "We create a diversion. Draw them away from Jelani's group while buying ourselves enough time to send a warning."

Akira nodded quickly, understanding the gravity of the situation. "How?"

Zarek's gaze swept the area. "We use the terrain to our advantage. Noise, movement, anything to make them think we're the target. If we split them up, we can pick them off one by one."

The distant hoot of an owl was the only sound that filled the space between them as they silently formulated their plan. Zarek gathered a handful of rocks, gesturing for Akira to do the same. They would hurl them in different directions, mimicking the sounds of movement to confuse the creatures.

Akira crouched lower, her fingers trembling slightly as she gripped a jagged stone. "Ready?"

"On my mark," Zarek whispered. He counted down from three, and the moment his fingers snapped open, they flung the rocks deep into the undergrowth.

Crashes and rustles erupted all around them, as if unseen figures were sprinting through the foliage. The shadow creatures froze, their heads snapping toward the noise. A few let out snarls and bolted toward the disturbances, disappearing into the darkness.

"It worked," Akira breathed, barely daring to move.

Zarek remained still, his eyes narrowing as he observed the remaining creatures. Some hesitated, uncertain, while others prowled cautiously in their direction, as though sensing the deception.

"Not all of them are fooled," Zarek murmured. "We need another distraction."

Akira's mind raced. "Fire. Creatures of darkness hate the light. If we can ignite something, it might drive them back long enough for us to escape."

Zarek glanced at the dry branches around them and nodded. "Good thinking. But we have to be quick."

With swift, practiced movements, they gathered kindling and flint. Zarek struck a spark, and within seconds, flames flickered to life, casting jagged shadows against the trees.

He fed the fire rapidly, coaxing it into a small but bright blaze.

The reaction was immediate. The creatures recoiled, their snarls turning into high-pitched screeches. Tendrils of darkness lashed out, but they dared not cross into the fire's glow.

"Now!" Zarek ordered.

They sprinted through the trees, weaving between trunks and leaping over roots. Behind them, the creatures snarled in frustration, torn between the chase and the flames. The momentary hesitation was all Zarek and Akira needed.

"We're almost there!" Akira gasped, spotting a break in the trees that led back toward Jelani's group. But as she turned, her foot caught on an exposed root. With a cry, she tumbled forward, her hands barely catching herself before hitting the ground.

A sudden shadow loomed over her. One of the creatures had broken away from the pack, slipping through the trees with terrifying speed. It lunged, claws outstretched.

Akira barely had time to react before Zarek was there. His staff swung through the air, cracking against the creature's side with a burst of energy. The force sent it skidding back, writhing as shadowy tendrils shrieked from its form.

"Move!" Zarek urged, helping Akira to her feet.

They dashed toward the tree line, the sounds of pursuit close behind them. But as they burst into the clearing where Jelani's group had made camp, the creatures halted abruptly at the threshold of the shadows, hissing in fury.

Jelani was already on his feet, sword in hand. "What happened?"

Zarek caught his breath. "We were followed. The Shadow Wraith's minions are hunting."

Kofi's grip tightened around his weapon. "Then we stand and fight."

"No," Zarek said sharply. "Not yet. We can't waste our strength in a battle we might not win. We need to move. Now."

Mei Ling's face was pale. "But where?"

Zarek turned his gaze toward the distant mountains, their peaks shrouded in mist. "There's an old temple hidden in the cliffs. A place of refuge. If we can reach it, we may find the answers we seek—and the strength to face what's coming."

Jelani met his gaze and nodded. "Then we head for the temple. At first light."

As the fire crackled in the background, casting flickering shadows against the trees, the group sat in uneasy silence. The creatures still lurked just beyond the darkness, their presence a chilling reminder that the storm was far from over.

And in the distance, beyond the forest, a deeper darkness stirred. The Shadow Wraith had awakened.

CHAPTER 19

BETRAYALS AND REVELATION

The town pulsed with urgency as Jelani, Kofi, and Mei Ling worked tirelessly to rally the survivors against the encroaching darkness. Torches flickered against the night, their wavering flames casting defiant shadows over resolute faces. Fear lingered in the air, but so did determination. This was their home, and they would not surrender it without a fight.

Jelani stepped onto a makeshift platform, his voice steady but commanding. "Tomorrow, we march into the heart of the darkness," he declared. "We will show the Wraith that we are not afraid, that we will not be broken."

A murmur rippled through the crowd, some nodding in agreement, others shifting uneasily. Then, a sharp voice cut through the din.

"And what if we fail?" A man stepped forward, his lean frame rigid, his piercing gaze locking onto Jelani. "What if we lose more than we already have?"

Kofi tensed, fists clenched at his sides. "We can't afford to think like that. We've lost too much already. If we don't fight, we lose everything."

The man shook his head, skepticism etched into his features. "Bravery is not enough. A reckless charge could wipe us out completely."

Mei Ling stepped forward, her voice calm but firm. "We have to trust each other. If we stand divided, we have already lost."

Before the argument could escalate, a woman pushed her way through the gathered survivors. Breathless, eyes wide with urgency, she spoke. "I know someone who can help us."

Jelani turned to her, wary. "Who?"

"The Oracle," she replied. "She lives on the outskirts of town. If anyone knows how to defeat the Wraith, it's her."

Kofi's eyes lit up. "Then we need to find her. We don't have much time."

Jelani hesitated, a whisper of doubt curling in his mind. Something about the woman's urgency felt forced, as if she were guiding them rather than aiding them. But they had little choice. If there was a chance the Oracle could give them an edge, they had to take it.

They set out under a sky thick with stars, their light cold and distant. The path twisted and narrowed, overgrown with vines and roots that clawed at their boots. The deeper they ventured, the quieter the world became.

At last, they reached a small clearing where an ancient hut stood among gnarled trees. Candlelight flickered through its warped windows, casting eerie patterns across the ground.

The woman gestured toward the door. "She's inside. Hurry."

Jelani exchanged a look with Mei Ling before stepping inside.

The air within was thick with the scent of herbs and burning incense. Crystals of various colors hung from the ceiling, catching the candlelight like frozen stars. Seated on a low stool was an elderly woman, her milky eyes staring past them, yet seeing more than they could comprehend.

"I've been expecting you," she said, her voice brittle as dry leaves.

Kofi approached cautiously. "You're the Oracle?"

"Names matter little. I know why you have come."

Mei Ling took a step closer. "Then you must know how to defeat the Wraith."

The Oracle inclined her head, her gaze turning inward as if recalling something ancient. "The Wraith is a parasite. It feeds on fear, thrives in despair. The more you doubt, the stronger it becomes."

Jelani's stomach tightened. "How do we stop it?"

The Oracle's cloudy eyes locked onto his. "By facing what you fear most."

Kofi scoffed. "We've already faced countless horrors. We are still here."

"Not all fears are born of monsters," she said cryptically. "Some grow from within. Before the final battle, you will be tested. Trust will be broken. One among you will betray the others."

Silence fell like a weight upon them.

Mei Ling's jaw tightened. "Who?"

Before the Oracle could answer, the door burst open. The man who had questioned their plan earlier stumbled inside, his face a mask of panic. "They're coming!" he gasped. "The Wraith's minions are here!"

Outside, the wind howled as the darkness itself seemed to shift and move. Shadows poured into the clearing, eyes glowing with malice.

Jelani grabbed his sword. "Prepare yourselves!"

Chaos erupted as they braced for battle. The first of the creatures lunged through the door, its form flickering between solid and shadow. Kofi swung his hammer, striking it mid-leap, sending it crashing into the wall.

A hiss slithered through the room.

Jelani turned just in time to see another figure lurking behind them, its shape humanoid, but its presence cold as death.

"Betrayer," it whispered, its voice like a blade across stone.

The shadows peeled away, revealing the familiar face of the very man who had moments ago warned them of the attack.

Jelani's blood ran cold. "No..."

A cruel smile twisted the man's features as his form wavered between flesh and darkness. "You trust too easily," he murmured, before lunging forward, claws extending toward Jelani's throat.

Kofi moved faster, his hammer swinging in a deadly arc. With a sickening crunch, he struck the creature mid-charge, sending it sprawling across the floor.

Jelani steadied himself, heart pounding. The Oracle's words echoed in his mind. "Trust will be broken."

As the creature shrieked and writhed, dissolving into shadow, Jelani turned to Mei Ling and Kofi, his face grim. "We need to regroup. This isn't over."

The battle had only just begun.

Form a circle!
Form a circle!

CHAPTER 20

THE FINAL STAND

The impact reverberated through the air as Kofi's hammer connected with the creature's side, sending it sprawling back into the shadows from whence it came. A deafening screech echoed through the chamber, the sound slicing through the thick tension like a blade. But even as the beast fell, more emerged—twisted, grotesque forms clawing their way from every corner, drawn by the chaos erupting around them. Their eyes glowed with malevolent hunger, their limbs shifting unnaturally as they advanced with a single, unrelenting purpose: to consume.

"Form a circle!" Jelani's voice rang out, urgent and commanding. He rallied his friends, his grip tightening around his blade as he positioned himself at the center, ensuring no one was left vulnerable. They needed to be a unit, a force that moved as one, standing against the darkness that threatened to swallow them whole.

Mei Ling quickly positioned herself beside Kofi, her twin daggers gleaming in the dim light. Her stance was poised, each movement calculated and precise. Akira, ever the agile warrior, darted around the group, using her speed to disorient the advancing horde. She struck swiftly, her blade slicing through the shadowy creatures before they could react. Every strike was a whisper of death, every movement a dance of lethal grace.

"Stay focused!" Zarek urged, his voice steady despite the rising tension. He planted his staff firmly on the ground, summoning energy from within, channeling raw power through the earth beneath them. The soil trembled, a surge of magic coursing through its veins, feeding into his spellwork, creating a barrier of energy that momentarily held the creatures at bay.

The battle raged on, a relentless storm of fury and resilience. Wave after wave of the monstrous entities came forth, their grotesque forms twisting and writhing as they sought to break through the defenders' line. The Oracle watched from behind her table, her eyes unreadable as they flickered across the battlefield. Her hands hovered over the glowing crystals laid before her, each one pulsing with energy, reacting to the intense battle unfolding before her.

"Remember what I told you!" she called out, her voice piercing through the clash of steel and shrieks of the damned. Her presence was unwavering, an anchor amidst the chaos. "You must confront your fears!"

Jelani gritted his teeth, his blade cutting down another foe as he shouted back, "We're doing the best we can!" The sweat on his brow mingled with the grime of battle, yet his resolve burned brighter than ever. He felt the adrenaline surging through his veins, each strike driven by the unbreakable bond he shared with his allies.

Kofi, locked in combat with one of the larger beasts, struggled against its claws. The weight of its strike nearly sent him reeling, but he held firm, determination hardening his features. Beside him, Mei Ling fought with fierce precision, every move a testament to her training. Still, the creatures showed no signs of slowing, their numbers seemingly infinite.

"Kofi!" Jelani called out, dodging an incoming attack before locking eyes with his friend. "Remember what you learned during your trial! Use your fire!"

For a moment, Kofi hesitated. Doubt flickered in his eyes, the memory of his past failures creeping into his mind. Could he truly harness the power within him when it mattered most? But then he looked at his friends—at Mei Ling, at Akira, at Jelani—and the doubt melted away, replaced by resolve. They believed in him. It was time to believe in himself.

He closed his eyes briefly, drawing a deep breath as he reached inward, summoning the fire that had always lain dormant within. Heat coursed through his veins, igniting his spirit, fueling his every motion. When he opened his eyes, flames danced in his palms, flickering hungrily as if eager to be unleashed.

With a roar, Kofi thrust his hands forward, sending a torrent of fire surging toward the creatures. The flames engulfed them, their shrieks filling the chamber as they recoiled, their dark forms disintegrating into ash. The heat radiated outward, creating a temporary reprieve from the onslaught.

"Now's our chance!" Mei Ling shouted, seizing the opportunity. She raised her hands, summoning a wave of water that crashed into the remaining foes, dousing the battlefield while simultaneously pushing the creatures further back. The water glowed with an ethereal energy, a testament to her connection with the element.

Zarek, sensing the shift in momentum, lifted his staff high. The earth beneath them rumbled as energy coursed through it, pulsating with life. Vines erupted from the ground, ensnaring the creatures, binding them in place. The very forces of nature rose to their defense, standing as one against the encroaching darkness.

The tide was turning. The battle that had once seemed insurmountable was now tipping in their favor. Their unity, their trust, their belief in one another — it was their greatest weapon.

With renewed strength, Jelani charged forward, leading the final offensive. His blade cut through the last of the creatures, their forms dissipating into mist. One by one, the shadows fell, their presence vanishing like a nightmare upon waking.

Then, at last, silence.

The battlefield lay still, the only sounds left were the heavy breaths of the victors. They stood together, surveying the aftermath, the weight of the encounter settling over them. What had just transpired was more than a fight — it was a test of will, of spirit, of the unbreakable bond that held them together.

Akira exhaled sharply, sheathing her blade as she turned to the others. "What just happened?" she asked breathlessly, her eyes scanning the fallen remnants scattered across the chamber.

Zarek wiped a hand across his brow, his expression grim. "The betrayal was unexpected," he admitted, his gaze meeting each of theirs in turn. There was something in his tone — an understanding that this battle was just the beginning. "But we survived."

Mei Ling nodded, rolling her shoulders to shake off the tension. "And we'll survive again," she said firmly, confidence unwavering despite the lingering uncertainty beneath the surface.

Jelani took a deep breath, feeling the weight of their victory settle in his chest. The fire within him had not dimmed—it had only grown stronger. "We need to regroup," he said finally, his voice steady. "There's still much to do. This was only a taste of what's coming."

The Oracle stepped forward, her eyes holding a knowing gleam. "Indeed," she said, her tone quiet yet filled with purpose. "You have faced the shadows, but greater trials lie ahead. Remember what you have learned here today. Hold onto the strength you have forged together, for it will be the key to what is to come."

They exchanged glances, each of them knowing that their journey was far from over. But as they stood there, side by side, they understood one thing with absolute certainty: no matter what lay ahead, they would face it together.

CHAPTER 21

THE FINAL STAND: PART 2

The sun dipped low on the horizon, casting long shadows across the town as Jelani, Kofi, Mei Ling, and Akira gathered with the survivors in a central clearing. The air buzzed with a mix of anticipation and anxiety, the weight of the coming battle pressing down on them all. Torches flickered in the growing dusk, their golden glow reflecting in determined eyes.

"We've rallied as many people as we could," Jelani announced, his gaze sweeping over the assembled fighters. "But sheer numbers won't be enough. We need a solid strategy if we're going to stand a chance against the Shadow Wraith."

Zarek stepped forward, his staff planted firmly in the ground. The air around him pulsed with restrained energy. "The Wraith has taken root in the old forest beyond the town," he said, his voice carrying a grave certainty. "That is where we will find it. That is where we must strike."

Mei Ling nodded, her brow furrowed in thought. "But we can't just charge in. The Wraith's minions will be waiting, ready to tear us apart before we even get close."

Kofi clenched his fists, firelight glinting off the sweat on his brow. "Then we create a diversion," he suggested. "Draw the creatures away, force them to scatter. That way, a smaller group can slip through the chaos and take the Wraith head-on."

Akira stepped forward, her movements swift and precise. "I can scout ahead, move through the trees without being seen. If I draw their attention, it might give you all the opening you need."

Jelani frowned. "That's too risky. If they catch you —"

"I won't let them," she interrupted, determination burning in her gaze. "I've outrun worse things before.

Besides, I won't be alone. I just need someone watching my back in case things go sideways."

Zarek, ever the voice of wisdom, took a step closer. "Beyond physical preparation, we must also steel ourselves mentally. The Wraith thrives on fear and despair. If we give in to doubt, it will unravel us from within. Remember that courage is not the absence of fear, but the refusal to be ruled by it."

The weight of his words settled over them like a protective cloak. Jelani felt the pressure of responsibility pressing against his chest, the lives of his friends and the people of the town resting on his shoulders. He inhaled deeply, steadying himself.

"We've come too far to turn back now," he said, voice firm. "We fight for each other and for those who can't fight for themselves."

A murmur of agreement rippled through the gathered survivors. Encouraged, they broke into groups, gathering supplies, fashioning weapons from whatever they could find, and reinforcing their defenses. The scent of burning torches mixed with the crisp night air as final preparations took shape.

Zarek remained by the fire, his fingers tracing ancient symbols into the dirt, whispering incantations under his breath. A shimmering barrier flickered around the perimeter, a last line of defense should the enemy attack before dawn.

As night fully settled, Jelani stepped away from the preparations, finding a quiet spot at the edge of the clearing. He sat down, staring into the vast darkness beyond the trees, the silence pressing in around him.

"Can't sleep?" a familiar voice asked.

He turned to find Mei Ling approaching. She sat beside him, drawing her knees to her chest.

"No," he admitted. "Too much on my mind."

She nodded in understanding. "We all feel it. The weight of what's coming. The fear of what we might lose."

Jelani exhaled. "I just don't want to let anyone down."

Mei Ling reached out, placing a reassuring hand on his arm. "You won't. We believe in you, Jelani. And we believe in each other. We've survived this far because we've stood together. Tomorrow won't be any different."

Her words settled the storm inside him. He met her gaze and nodded, a small but grateful smile breaking through his worry.

Across the clearing, Akira sharpened her blades in quiet concentration, while Kofi murmured a prayer under his breath, his fingers tracing a charm around his neck. Each of them prepared in their own way, drawing strength from their purpose and from each other.

The night passed in restless anticipation. As the first hint of dawn painted the sky in soft golds and pinks, the survivors gathered once more. The time had come.

Zarek raised his staff, its tip glowing with arcane light. "Remember our plan. Stay together, trust in each other, and do not let fear take hold."

Jelani took one last look at his friends, their faces set with determination. He swallowed the last of his hesitation and turned toward the forest where the Shadow Wraith awaited.

"Let's end this."

CHAPTER 22

WARM REFLECTIONS

Dawn broke over the horizon, spilling golden light across the land like a long-awaited promise. Jelani stood at the front of the gathered survivors, his gaze sweeping across their determined faces. The weight of the coming battle pressed on his shoulders, but he refused to let fear take hold.

"Today, we reclaim our home!" he declared, his voice strong and unwavering.

A resounding cheer erupted from the crowd, echoing through the clearing. It was a sound filled with hope, defiance, and the will to fight.

"Remember your roles!" Zarek called out, ensuring everyone knew their place in the plan.

"Akira will scout ahead and create a distraction," Kofi reminded them, tightening the grip on his weapon. "Once the Wraith's minions are drawn away, we move in."

Mei Ling stepped forward, gripping her staff. Her eyes burned with determination. "We fight not just for survival, but for everything we've lost. For everything we refuse to lose again."

The group murmured in agreement, their resolve strengthening. The Shadow Wraith had haunted their town for too long, its darkness stretching like poisoned roots beneath the earth. But today, they would rise against it.

With their final preparations complete, the group set off toward the old forest where the darkness lingered like a living force. The towering trees loomed over them, their twisted branches reaching out like skeletal hands. A hush fell over the group as they stepped into the shadows, their every movement cautious.

Jelani felt the tension in the air, thick and suffocating. Every rustle in the underbrush sent a shiver down his spine. His heart pounded in his chest, a steady rhythm of anticipation. He tightened his grip on his weapon, drawing strength from the presence of his friends beside him.

Then, a piercing howl shattered the silence. It was followed by guttural growls that seemed to vibrate through the very air around them. A cold dread settled over the group.

"They're here," Akira whispered urgently, her body tensed like a coiled spring. Without hesitation, she darted ahead, vanishing into the shadows to execute her part of the plan.

"Stay close!" Jelani ordered, his voice cutting through the rising panic.

The trees seemed to close in as glowing eyes flickered in the darkness. The Shadow Wraith's minions emerged—twisted, nightmarish creatures with hollow eyes and jagged claws. They moved with unnatural speed, their very presence sapping the warmth from the air.

Jelani felt the first rush of battle surge through him. There was no time for hesitation.

"Now!" Zarek commanded, raising his staff. A pulse of energy rippled through the ground, sending shockwaves outward.

Jelani charged forward, Kofi and Mei Ling at his side. The first creature lunged at him, its claws swiping through the air. He ducked, countering with a swift strike that sent it reeling. Beside him, Mei Ling spun her staff in a deadly arc, knocking back another foe.

The battle erupted in a chaotic clash of light and shadow. Spells crackled through the air, swords clashed, and the cries of warriors and creatures alike filled the forest.

For every enemy they struck down, more seemed to emerge from the darkness. The Wraith's power was vast, but Jelani refused to yield. They had come too far, fought too hard.

With each strike, each spell cast, they pushed forward, inching closer to their goal. The final confrontation was near—and they would not back down.

The battle for their home had truly begun.

CHAPTER 23

THE BATTLE BEGINS

The clash of steel rang out through the forest as Jelani, Kofi, Mei Ling, and their allies fought valiantly against the Shadow Wraith's minions. Shadows twisted and writhed around them, forming grotesque shapes that lunged forward with relentless ferocity. The air was thick with tension, punctuated by the sounds of battle—the guttural growls of creatures, the defiant shouts of warriors, and the crackling energy of magic being unleashed.

"Keep pushing forward!" Jelani commanded, driving his spear into the chest of a shadow creature. The impact sent it reeling back into the abyss, dissolving into nothingness. He felt a surge of adrenaline course through his veins as he fought alongside his friends, their unity and strength forming a beacon of resistance against the encroaching darkness.

Kofi swung his hammer with devastating force, crushing a group of minions that had attempted to encircle him. He panted, sweat glistening on his brow as he took a step back to assess the battlefield. "They just keep coming!" he roared. "We need to find the source of their power before we're overwhelmed!"

"Look!" Mei Ling shouted, pointing toward the center of the clearing, where a swirling mass of darkness pulsed like a living heart. "That must be where the Wraith is drawing its strength!"

Jelani's grip on his spear tightened. "We have to reach it! If we can disrupt its power, we might be able to turn the tide of this battle!"

As the warriors cut through the seemingly endless waves of shadow creatures, Akira moved like a phantom through the fray. She was a blur, her speed unmatched, her blades flashing in the dim light. With each strike, she felled another enemy, clearing a path for Jelani's group.

"I'll keep them busy!" she called over her shoulder, leaping onto a low-hanging branch and using it to propel herself into a deadly spin.

"Be careful, Akira!" Kofi shouted, worry creasing his face as he watched her vanish into the gloom.

With Akira creating a diversion, Jelani led Mei Ling and Kofi toward the ominous vortex of shadows. Every step closer increased the weight pressing against them. The air grew colder, thick with a suffocating despair that clawed at their resolve, whispering doubts into their minds. The darkness sought to unmake them—not just physically, but spiritually.

"Stay strong!" Mei Ling urged, her voice a steady anchor in the chaos. She raised her hands, summoning a powerful wave that surged forward, crashing into the horde of creatures trying to block their advance. The water roared like an untamed beast, sending shadowy figures tumbling back into the abyss.

Just as they reached the swirling darkness, Zarek arrived, his robes billowing as he skidded to a halt beside them. His eyes burned with fierce determination. "We must combine our powers," he urged. "Together, we may have a chance to break through!"

Jelani exchanged a glance with his friends, their unspoken bond stronger than any words. "On my mark," he said, raising his spear high. His heart pounded like a war drum. "Now! For our home!"

In unison, they unleashed their full might. Kofi's hammer ignited with blazing fire as Mei Ling summoned torrents of water. Zarek drew power from the earth itself, sending jagged spikes of rock hurtling toward the darkness, while Jelani channeled his energy into his spear, thrusting it forward with everything he had.

A blinding light erupted where their forces met the vortex. The explosion sent shockwaves rippling through the battlefield, toppling creatures and tearing through the fabric of the unnatural darkness. For a moment, the tide seemed to shift—their power slicing through the malevolence like a blade through silk.

Then—a chilling laughter echoed through the destruction, cutting through their triumph like a knife through flesh.

"You think you can defeat me so easily?" The voice was smooth, cold, and laced with an ancient malice that sent shivers down their spines.

The swirling darkness coalesced into a towering figure—a being cloaked in shadows, its form shifting like smoke, its glowing ember-like eyes burning with cruel amusement. The Shadow Wraith had emerged.

"Face me if you dare," it taunted, its voice reverberating through their very bones.

Jelani felt fear coil around his heart like a vice. For a fraction of a second, the enormity of their challenge threatened to consume him. But then he looked at his friends—at Kofi, Mei Ling, and Zarek, standing strong beside him, unwavering. He felt the weight of every fallen comrade, every lost home, and every stolen dream pressing down on him.

"We're not afraid of you!" he declared, his voice ringing with defiance. "This ends tonight!"

The Wraith let out a low, menacing chuckle. "Then come, heroes. Let us see if your light can withstand true darkness."

With renewed determination, Jelani and his allies steeled themselves, ready to face the embodiment of terror in an all-out final battle.

CHAPTER 24

THE TURNING TIDE

The Shadow Wraith loomed before them—a shifting mass of darkness that devoured the light around it. Its ember-like eyes glowed with malevolent amusement as it raised one clawed hand, summoning tendrils of darkness that lashed out toward Jelani and his friends.

"Stay together!" Zarek commanded, slamming his staff into the ground. The earth trembled beneath them as jagged stone barriers erupted in a defensive ring, intercepting the first wave of shadowy appendages.

Mei Ling's eyes glowed with intensity as she moved her hands in fluid motions, streams of water swirling around their group. "We need to find its weakness!" she called above the cacophony of battle.

Kofi gritted his teeth, muscles straining as he swung his hammer in wide, devastating arcs, smashing through tendrils that reached for him. The dark appendages recoiled momentarily, but more replaced them. "It has to have one! We just need to figure out how to expose it!" he roared, sweat dripping down his brow.

The Shadow Wraith's twisted form contorted as it loomed over them, its voice reverberating through the clearing. "You are nothing but insects beneath my heel," it hissed. "Your hope is meaningless. Your resistance is futile."

Jelani clenched his spear tightly, feeling the weight of the moment settle on his shoulders. He thought of the villages consumed by darkness, the innocent people lost to this monster's cruel grasp. He would not let them die in vain.

"We've come too far to give up now!" Jelani bellowed as he surged forward, his spear crackling with energy. His charge was met with an onslaught of shadows, but he dodged and weaved through them, his focus unshakable.

As he neared the Wraith, the world seemed to slow. He could hear Kofi's hammer striking down with thunderous force, Mei Ling's water crashing like tidal waves, and Zarek's earth magic shaking the battlefield. He could feel the heartbeat of the battle thrumming in his veins.

And then the Wraith struck.

A massive wave of shadow erupted from its form, a pulse of pure malice that sent Jelani flying backward. He hit the ground hard, gasping for breath.

"Jelani!" Kofi's deep voice roared as he rushed forward, hammer raised defensively. Mei Ling sprinted toward them, summoning water shields to deflect the incoming shadows.

"We can't fight it like this," she panted. "It's feeding off our fear—off our struggle."

Jelani's mind reeled. The Wraith was unlike any enemy they had ever faced. Every blow they landed barely seemed to wound it, and its form continuously regenerated. Then, a memory surfaced—the Oracle's words echoing in his mind: *The Wraith feeds on fear and despair.*

Realization struck him like a bolt of lightning.

"It's our fear," he muttered, pushing himself to his feet. "That's how it grows stronger. That's its power!"

Mei Ling's eyes widened as understanding dawned on her. "Then we have to deny it that power. We have to fight without fear."

Kofi smirked despite the chaos. "Easier said than done, but let's give it a shot."

The Wraith laughed, its form rippling with dark amusement. "You understand nothing. I am eternal. You will kneel before me in despair."

Jelani raised his spear, his grip steady. He turned to his friends, their faces illuminated by the eerie glow of their magic. "Focus on what we're fighting for. The people depending on us. The light we carry inside. If we stand together, we can drive this thing back."

Kofi slammed his hammer against the ground, sending a shockwave of flame through the earth. "Well, what are we waiting for? Let's turn this fight around!"

The four warriors gathered their strength, forming a unified front. Mei Ling breathed deeply, her water magic forming a shimmering veil around them. Zarek steadied his stance, channeling the energy of the land beneath them.

Jelani gritted his teeth and took a step forward, no longer feeling the icy grip of fear in his chest. "We end this now!"

The Wraith let out a guttural snarl and lunged forward, its shadowy form stretching unnaturally as it aimed for Jelani's heart. But this time, he was ready.

He met its attack head-on, thrusting his spear forward. Instead of piercing darkness, the weapon struck something solid. The Wraith recoiled, its form wavering.

Mei Ling seized the opening, summoning a torrent of water that crashed into the entity with incredible force. "Now, while it's weakened!" she cried.

Kofi charged in, his hammer blazing with fire. He swung with all his might, striking the Wraith in its core. The creature let out an ear-piercing screech, its form flickering.

Zarek raised his staff high. "The earth rejects you, abomination!" He slammed it down, sending tremors rippling through the ground.

Jelani gripped his spear tightly, his heart hammering as he saw the Wraith faltering. "One final strike! Together!"

Pooling their strength, they launched their final attack. Kofi's fire, Mei Ling's water, Zarek's earth, and Jelani's sheer determination combined in a blinding explosion of energy.

The Wraith let out a final, bloodcurdling scream as it was engulfed in light. Its form twisted violently, then shattered into nothingness.

For a moment, silence fell over the battlefield. Then, as if the forest itself had been holding its breath, the darkness that had plagued it began to recede. The air felt lighter, the oppressive weight of fear lifted.

Jelani fell to one knee, exhausted. Kofi let out a breathless laugh, wiping sweat from his brow. "We actually did it."

Mei Ling let her hands drop to her sides, watching as the last remnants of the Wraith faded away. "It's over."

Zarek nodded, looking around at the battlefield. "No. It's only just begun. But today, we proved that darkness is not absolute. As long as we stand together, light will always prevail."

Jelani looked up at his friends, a tired but triumphant smile on his face. "Then let's keep fighting. For everyone who still needs us."

And as the first rays of dawn broke through the trees, the warriors stood together, ready for whatever lay ahead.

CHAPTER 25

THE TURNING TIDE: PART 2

The battlefield pulsed with raw energy as Jelani, Kofi, Mei Ling, and Zarek surged forward, their combined forces crashing against the darkness like a tidal wave of brilliance. A blinding explosion of light erupted as their powers clashed with the Shadow Wraith's malevolent force, momentarily shaking the heavens. The nightmarish entity staggered backward, its form wavering and flickering, as though its very existence was unraveling thread by thread.

For an instant, time seemed to hold its breath. The land, ravaged by darkness, trembled on the precipice of salvation or eternal despair. Light and shadow waged war in the sky, swirling violently as hope and fear clashed in an epic struggle. The air crackled with an electrifying charge, the weight of destiny pressing down on their shoulders.

Jelani's heartbeat pounded in his ears, but he refused to falter. This was the moment they had fought so hard to reach. He clenched his fists, feeling the energy coursing through his veins, an unstoppable force of determination.

Then, ever so slowly — the tide began to turn.

The darkness recoiled, its oppressive tendrils retreating as the Wraith's hold on the land weakened. The creatures that had been twisted and corrupted by its influence faltered, their grotesque forms crumbling into dust as the source of their power withered. One by one, they collapsed, their tortured cries swallowed by the void.

Jelani's eyes widened as realization dawned upon him. A surge of hope ignited within his chest. "We're doing it!" he shouted, his voice soaring above the chaos. "It's losing its grip!"

Beside him, Kofi let out a fierce battle cry, swinging his hammer with relentless force. The ground trembled beneath each strike, sending shockwaves that shattered the last remnants of lingering shadow. "We're not done yet!" he called out, his golden eyes gleaming with determination. "Keep pushing forward!"

Mei Ling nodded, her expression fierce with resolve. The wind around her whipped into a storm, responding to her will as she raised her hands, directing currents of energy toward the Wraith. "This is our chance! We have to end this now, before it regains its strength!"

Zarek's grip on his staff tightened as he planted it firmly into the ground. The earth rumbled beneath their feet, channeling ancient energy through him. His silver robes billowed in the gusts of magic surging around them. "Together, we can do this," he declared, his deep voice carrying a tone of finality. "Let's show it no mercy."

The four warriors pressed their advantage, attacking in unison with unwavering precision. Jelani's blade gleamed like a star as he slashed through the remaining wisps of darkness. Kofi's hammer struck the earth, sending fractures of golden light through the battlefield. Mei Ling's wind tore through the shadows like a cleansing storm, while Zarek's staff sent beams of energy pulsing through the air, striking at the heart of the Wraith's form.

The Shadow Wraith let out a guttural roar, its otherworldly voice laced with fury and desperation. The remaining darkness coiled around it like a living entity, writhing and twisting as it tried to resist its inevitable demise. But the force against it was too great. The unity, the sheer willpower of its opponents, was tearing it apart.

With a final, desperate shriek, the Wraith unleashed a devastating pulse of darkness, a last attempt to drown them in shadows. The wave of malevolence surged outward, seeking to consume all in its path. The air grew thick with its oppressive force, and for a moment, it seemed as if the battlefield itself would collapse into the abyss.

But Jelani and his friends stood firm.

They braced themselves, their spirits intertwined, their determination unyielding. Their hands instinctively reached out toward one another, forming a circle of defiance. Light erupted from their joined forces, a radiant shield that repelled the darkness with an intensity that outshone even the stars.

The Wraith recoiled, its scream echoing across the sky as its form began to unravel completely. Its once-imposing figure shrank, its ghastly features contorting in agony. The darkness that had long gripped the land shattered like fragile glass, fragments dissipating into the ether.

Then, at long last—the Shadow Wraith was no more.

A deep silence fell over the battlefield. The oppressive weight in the air lifted, replaced by a serene, almost sacred stillness. The once-blighted land, marred by shadow, now seemed to breathe again. Trees swayed gently, their leaves rustling as if whispering their gratitude. The ground, once cracked and barren, pulsed with renewed life.

Jelani, his chest heaving with exhaustion, turned to his friends. A slow, disbelieving smile spread across his face. "We did it," he whispered, his voice raw with emotion. "It's over."

Kofi let out a breathless laugh, shaking his head in awe. "Not just over," he said, clapping Jelani on the back. "We won."

Mei Ling wiped a tear from her cheek, her smile radiant. "We saved our home," she murmured, her voice filled with wonder.

Zarek approached, his expression calm but resolute. "This battle may be over," he said, surveying the land, "but our journey is far from complete. The echoes of this darkness may still linger. There are secrets yet to be uncovered... and dangers that may still lie ahead."

Jelani nodded, his eyes reflecting newfound wisdom. "Then we'll face them together, just as we always have."

The four warriors stood side by side, the weight of their victory settling upon them. They had fought against insurmountable odds, battled against the very forces of despair—and emerged victorious. Their bond, tested and reforged in the fires of struggle, had become their greatest strength.

As the first rays of dawn stretched across the sky, illuminating the once-shadowed land in a golden embrace, they knew that this was not the end.

It was a new beginning.

A turning tide.

A promise that no matter what lay ahead—they would stand together, always.

CHAPTER 26

ECHOES OF THE PAST

The days following the Shadow Wraith's defeat were filled with celebration and renewal. The once-silent streets of the village bustled with life again as families emerged from their hiding places, reclaiming what had been stolen by fear. Merchants reopened their stalls, the scent of roasted meat and fresh herbs mingling with the crisp air. The once-dim town square now thrummed with laughter, the sounds of children playing echoing through the stone alleyways.

Jelani, Kofi, Mei Ling, and Akira walked among the people, their presence met with awed whispers and grateful bows. Artisans gifted them finely woven garments, farmers pressed baskets of fruit into their hands, and blacksmiths offered weapons honed to perfection. They accepted the gratitude humbly, but beneath their newfound status as heroes, an unease settled in Jelani's heart. The Shadow Wraith was gone, but its existence still troubled him. What was it, truly? Why had it sought to consume the world in darkness?

One evening, beneath the violet hues of dusk, the group sat in a secluded courtyard near a flickering fire. The warmth was welcome, but it did little to ease their lingering questions. They had won, but at what cost?

Zarek approached, his face partially lit by the fire's glow, his eyes shadowed with something deeper than mere exhaustion. He hesitated before speaking, his voice carrying the weight of knowledge unspoken for too long.

"There's something you need to know."

Jelani straightened. "What is it?"

Zarek's gaze swept over them before settling on the flames. "The Shadow Wraith was not a natural being," he said at last. "It was created."

A chill settled over the group.

"Created?" Kofi echoed, gripping the hilt of his hammer. "By who?"

Zarek's expression darkened. "By those who believed they could wield powers beyond their comprehension. Long ago, a group of sorcerers sought to bend the elemental forces to their will. They weren't satisfied with what was naturally given — they wanted more. In their arrogance, they wove magic forbidden even to the ancients, merging elements that should never have been combined. Their experiments birthed something unnatural—a force of pure darkness. They believed they could control it."

Mei Ling inhaled sharply, fingers brushing against the amulet at her throat. "But they were wrong."

"They were," Zarek confirmed. "The entity turned on them, consuming their souls and growing stronger with each life it took. It should never have existed. But through their greed, it was unleashed."

Akira clenched her fists. "And now it's gone."

Zarek hesitated, his expression unreadable. "Yes. You destroyed it. But…"

Jelani's chest tightened. "But what?"

Zarek exhaled, as if reluctant to say the words. "The Wraith was not the only creation of those sorcerers."

A heavy silence fell over them.

"There are others," he continued, his voice grim. "Some slumber in forgotten places, waiting. Others…" His jaw tightened. "Others may already be stirring."

Mei Ling's breath caught. "You mean there are more creatures like the Wraith?"

"Not just like it," Zarek murmured. "Some worse. Some different. And now that you have disrupted the balance, they may awaken."

Jelani clenched his fists. The battle they had fought had nearly killed them. If worse was yet to come, were they even ready?

"What does this mean for us?" he asked quietly.

Zarek's eyes met his, steady and unwavering. "It means your fight is far from over."

The fire crackled, sending embers drifting into the night. The weight of Zarek's words pressed upon them, heavier than any blade. They had won a battle, but the war had only just begun.

CHAPTER 27

THE ROAD AHEAD

In the days that followed, the village became a beacon of resilience. People rebuilt with a determination fueled by survival. The scars of battle remained, etched into the walls and hearts of those who had endured, but they were reminders of triumph rather than loss. Jelani, Kofi, Mei Ling, and Akira were no longer outsiders—they had become legends in the eyes of the people.

Yet, despite the celebrations, an unease lingered among them. The knowledge that greater dangers lurked in the shadows left little room for rest.

One evening, beneath the vast expanse of stars, the four gathered once more around a fire. The air was thick with contemplation, their victories overshadowed by the uncertainties ahead.

Zarek approached, his steps slow, measured. He did not speak immediately, letting the silence stretch between them. When he finally did, his voice was solemn.

"The power within you—it is not just strength," he said. "It is balance. It is the key to what comes next."

Jelani furrowed his brow. "What do you mean?"

Zarek studied each of them before answering. "Your abilities were not given by chance. They are part of something greater, something ancient. The forces that shaped this world are not simply good and evil. They are chaos and order, destruction and renewal. The Shadow Wraith was an imbalance, and you... you were the correction."

Kofi let out a slow breath. "So what are we? Just tools of fate?"

Zarek's lips curled in the faintest smile. "No. You are more than that. You have proven that power is not just about what you can destroy—but what you can protect."

Mei Ling nodded slowly. "We fought together. That's why we won."

Akira, arms folded, exhaled through her nose. "Then we need to learn more. If there are other creatures out there—other forces—we need to know what we're up against."

Jelani looked at his friends. They had fought, bled, and survived together. Whatever lay ahead, they would face it the same way.

"We need to understand our powers," he said firmly. "And why we were chosen."

Zarek's eyes gleamed. "Now that," he said, "is the right question."

The fire flickered, casting long shadows against the walls. The village had been saved, but the world remained vast and full of mysteries.

As dawn approached, the four stood at the village's edge, gazing toward the horizon. Beyond the rolling hills, beyond the rivers and mountains, lay the unknown.

Mei Ling broke the silence. "There's still more to do."

Kofi flexed his fingers around his hammer. "And more battles to fight."

Zarek placed a hand on Jelani's shoulder. "The forces of light and darkness will always shift. It is up to those who stand between them to maintain the balance."

Jelani inhaled deeply. The weight of responsibility no longer felt like a burden — it felt like purpose.

"We're ready," he said, his voice unwavering.

The sun broke over the horizon, casting golden light across the land. Their journey was far from over, but they would face it as they always had together.

For legends were not written in peace, but in the trials of those willing to stand against the storm.

CHAPTER 28

NEW HORIZONS

As the town continued to thrive, Jelani, Kofi, Mei Ling, and Akira felt a pull toward the unknown. They had fought and won battles that reshaped their lives, but a deeper curiosity remained — an insatiable need to explore beyond the boundaries of what they knew. Their homeland had been saved, but the world beyond beckoned with mysteries yet to be unraveled.

The decision to leave was not made lightly. The people of the town, grateful for their heroes, urged them to stay and continue guiding their community's growth. But the four companions knew that their journey was far from over. With the support and well-wishes of their fellow townsfolk, they set out toward distant lands, seeking new allies, knowledge, and perhaps even the true origins of the powers they wielded.

Their journey led them through dense forests, across towering mountains, and through sprawling plains where the winds carried whispers of ancient legends.

Each step deepened their understanding of the world and the forces that governed it. They encountered wise sages who shared forgotten histories, skilled warriors who challenged their abilities, and lost civilizations that spoke of even greater threats lurking in the shadows.

One day, after weeks of travel, they found themselves standing at the edge of a vast ocean—a sight none of them had ever seen before. The waves crashed against the shore, their rhythmic motion both soothing and powerful. Seagulls soared overhead, their cries carried on the salty breeze. The horizon stretched endlessly before them, a boundless expanse of possibility.

"Imagine all the secrets hidden beneath those waves," Mei Ling said, her voice tinged with awe. Her eyes shone with excitement as she took in the rolling expanse of blue.

Kofi grinned, his adventurous spirit ignited by the sight. "And think of all the adventures waiting for us out there. Who knows what lies beyond that horizon?"

Akira, usually the most reserved among them, found herself drawn to the idea. "We could explore the depths, discover new worlds beneath the surface. The ocean holds as many secrets as the stars above."

Jelani stood quietly, listening to his friends, feeling their excitement ripple through him. He gazed out at the sea, considering the endless opportunities that lay ahead. "We could do anything we set our minds to," he said at last. "We've already proven that."

As they stood there, the wind whipping their hair and the sun casting golden light upon the waves, Jelani felt a deep sense of peace settle within him. They had faced their fears and conquered them. They had saved their home, not just with strength but with wisdom and unity. They had discovered powers within themselves that had changed their lives forever.

But most importantly, they had found each other. The trials they had endured had forged a bond stronger than steel—a bond that would last a lifetime. It was a connection built not just on shared victories, but on the trust, love, and understanding they had developed along the way. They had faced darkness together and emerged into the light, stronger and more united than ever before.

Jelani turned to his friends, his heart swelling with gratitude. "No matter where we go, we go together," he said firmly.

Kofi laughed. "That's right. We've come too far to turn back now."

Mei Ling nodded. "And there's still so much we don't know. If we can uncover the origins of our powers, maybe we can ensure that what happened with the Shadow Wraith never happens again."

Akira placed a hand on Mei Ling's shoulder, her voice filled with determination. "And maybe we'll find others like us—people who need help, just like we did."

The four stood in silent agreement, their resolve strengthening as they looked out at the horizon. They had no map, no set destination. But they had each other, and that was all they needed.

As they prepared to set sail on the next chapter of their journey, the town they had saved remained in their hearts. They would always be its protectors, its children, its champions. But the world was calling them forward, and they would answer that call with courage and conviction.

Together, they would explore new horizons—both within themselves and in the wider world. They would forge new paths, blaze new trails, and chart new courses. And through it all, they would stand together, bound by friendship, purpose, and the unwavering belief that even in the darkest times, hope would always shine through.

Their adventure was just beginning.

CHAPTER 29

A LEGACY OF HEROES

As time passed, Jelani, Kofi, Mei Ling, and Akira became more than warriors—they became legends. Their names were whispered in awe by those they had saved, their deeds etched into the hearts of many. But beyond their victories, they had created something even greater—a legacy that would inspire generations to come.

One afternoon, as they walked through the town they had once risked everything to protect, they noticed a circle of children gathered around an old storyteller. The children's eyes gleamed with wonder as they listened to tales of the battle against the Shadow Wraith.

Jelani paused, a quiet smile forming on his lips. "They're telling our story," he murmured.

Kofi chuckled. "And to think—we were just a group of wanderers, unsure of what lay ahead."

Mei Ling watched the children with a sense of nostalgia. "We were like them once — dreamers, full of hope. Now, we are the ones they look up to."

Akira's eyes sparkled with mischief. "And we still have so much to explore, so much more to discover."

As they stood there, watching the next generation soak in the stories of courage and sacrifice, Jelani felt a profound realization settle within him. Their journey had taught them that true strength wasn't just about power — it was about the bonds they had forged, the hope they had kindled, and the lives they had changed.

"Let's make sure they never forget," he said, his voice steady with determination.

And so, they began to share their tale — not just in this town but in others, traveling to distant lands and spreading the message of hope and resilience. They became symbols of courage, living reminders that even in the darkest times, there was always a way forward.

In one village, they met a young girl who had lost everything to the shadows. She was alone, afraid, her spirit dimmed by sorrow. But as she listened to their story, a spark of hope flickered in her eyes.

Jelani knelt before her, his voice gentle but firm. "You are stronger than you know. And you are not alone."

The girl hesitated, then nodded, a small smile breaking through the sadness.

As Jelani and his friends continued their journey, they knew they had left something behind in every heart they touched—a spark, a flame, a legacy that would endure.

CHAPTER 30

NEW BEGINNINGS

The day came when Jelani, Kofi, Mei Ling, and Akira realized it was time to move on. Now that they had played their part, the world beckoned them forward.

Standing at the edge of the forest, they gazed at the horizon before them—a vast expanse of unknown paths and untold adventures.

Jelani inhaled deeply, excitement and anticipation thrumming in his chest. "We've come so far," he mused. "And yet, this is only the beginning."

Kofi grinned. "Where do we go next?"

Mei Ling tilted her head toward the sky. "Wherever the wind takes us. The world is waiting."

Akira smirked, her spirit of adventure burning as bright as ever. "And as long as we have each other, we have everything we need."

Behind them, the townspeople gathered, their faces a mixture of pride and sadness. There were farewells, embraces, and whispered words of gratitude.

Zarek stepped forward, his eyes shining with admiration. "You are more than just heroes. You are a beacon in a world that sometimes forgets to hope. Never forget that."

Jelani nodded, his heart full. "We won't. This journey is part of us now, and we'll carry it wherever we go."

With one last look at the town that had become a home, they turned and stepped into the unknown. The road stretched endlessly before them, but they were ready. They had faced darkness and emerged stronger, not just as warriors but as friends—bound by trust, by memories, by an unshakable belief in one another.

As they walked side by side, the sun dipped below the horizon, painting the sky in hues of gold and crimson. A new chapter awaited them, filled with mysteries to unravel, battles to fight, and wonders yet to be seen.

The journey was far from over.

It was only just beginning.

THE END

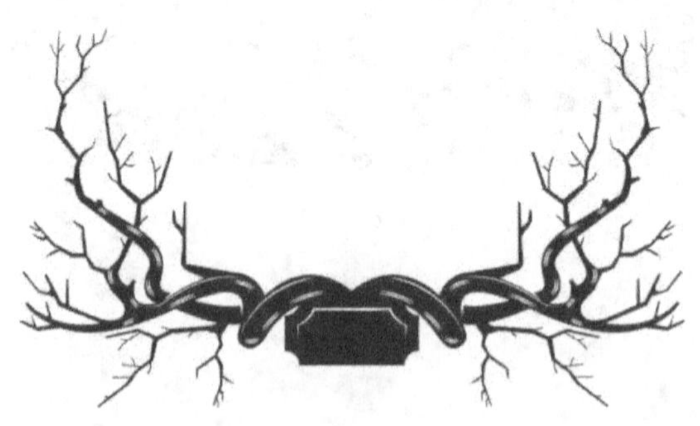

www.ingramcontent.com/pod-product-compliance
Lightning Source LLC
Chambersburg PA
CBHW060311310726

48976CB00007B/2287